SWEET FIRE

Into The Fire Series

J.H. CROIX

J.H. CROIX

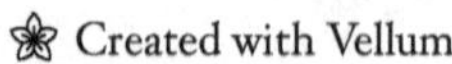 Created with Vellum

A toast to the complications of life, which make it all the richer.

Sign up for my newsletter for information on new releases & get a FREE copy of one of my books!

http://jhcroixauthor.com/subscribe/

Follow me!
jhcroix@jhcroix.com
https://amazon.com/author/jhcroix
https://www.bookbub.com/authors/j-h-croix
https://www.facebook.com/jhcroix

SWEET FIRE

Jesse

Dr. Lane is all kinds of uptight—oh-so proper and professional. I can't help but try to rile her up. I want her, and I can't even say why.

One night with her, and she's seared into my soul. All bets are off. But her life is complicated. I don't do complicated. So I think.

Because, you see, Charlie is everything I ever wanted and more. I just didn't know it yet. She was mine the minute I laid eyes on her.

Charlie

I don't believe in fairytales. I sure as h*ll don't have time for them. I also don't have time for Jesse Franklin—hotshot firefighter, too handsome for his own good, and cocky to boot.

He's also rude. Whatever. As I said, I don't have time. My life is complicated and messy. There is zero room for anything, most certainly not Jesse who I can't seem to kick out of my mind.

Then, he goes and does something I never expected. Ever. My life suddenly gets more complicated, and this time it's all about a fairytale.

Chapter One

JESSE

"Did you just tell me to go to hell?" Dr. Lane asked without even looking up from the screen on the small computer tablet she held.

Total fail at keeping my thoughts to myself. Dr. Lane finally looked up, pushing her glasses up on her nose as she did.

"I guess I did," I finally said with a sheepish smile. "I can't believe you're making me wait another two weeks before clearing me for full duty."

She cocked her head to the side from where she sat on a rolling stool by the counter. Her gray eyes scanned my face, and I wondered what the hell she was thinking. She was so fucking uptight.

I was at a doctor's appointment for a follow up after I'd had some tendon problems in my shoulder. I'd dislocated it a few months back and maybe, just maybe, didn't take it easy long enough. Dr. Lane was a new doctor in Willow Brook. I was used to Dr. Johnson, or Doc as I called him, a rather cantankerous older man who definitely wasn't as uptight.

I shifted my shoulders, thinking Dr. Lane could loosen

up. For God's sake, the woman wore her hair in a bun. I had no idea what her body looked like because she was always shrouded in a white lab coat. I suspected she had a banging body, or at least my cock thought so. Every damn time I saw her, I got tense — all over.

I rolled my offending shoulder, ignoring the slight twinge of soreness. "Helen said it was fine and I might be ready to be cleared," I explained, referring to my physical therapist.

Dr. Lane was not nearly as warm and friendly as Helen. My physical therapist had a grandmotherly warmth to her and made me feel better every time I saw her. Unlike Dr. Lane who made me feel tense and irritable. If only she would clear me to return to full duty, maybe I could relax.

Dr. Lane adjusted her glasses again, turning her head slightly as she set the computer tablet on the counter. As she turned, I noticed for the first time that she had a streak of purple in her dark hair. I did *not* know what to make of that.

Before I had much time to contemplate the implications of said purple streak, she spoke. "I could, but honestly that tendon got irritated because you probably pushed too fast last time. If you wait a little longer this time, you probably won't have the same problem again. I know you're frustrated with me, but I actually do have your best interests at heart."

I bit back another curse. Even if she made me tense, I wasn't an asshole and prone to telling women to go to hell. I took a deep breath and ran a hand through my hair as I let my breath out in a sigh. I might've been annoyed, but I wasn't an idiot. "Fine. I get your point. Helen said the same thing. She's just a little easier to persuade than you," I said, flashing a grin.

I couldn't say why, but that streak of purple relaxed me. I supposed it cued me to the fact Dr. Lane might not be as uptight as I'd assumed. Dr. Lane's lips twitched, but she didn't say anything. Something about her made me want to ruffle her feathers. Big time.

Except for days like today, the only other times I'd seen

her had been on the heels of a shift when I was dirty and grimy from dealing with a fire. Perhaps that was why she set me off—the contrast of her tidy form in comparison to mine. I was a hotshot firefighter, so when I came in after a day's work, I was about the complete opposite of tidy. It also annoyed me to no end to deal with injuries.

"So you don't mind waiting another two weeks?" she asked.

I shrugged, my shoulder giving a slight twinge as I did, which should've been my cue that waiting was smart. I was bored out of my fucking mind being off of duty. It wasn't that I couldn't work. There was plenty to do, but I was relegated to light duty tasks when I preferred to throw myself into work. I loved my job as a firefighter. I loved the hard work and the physical challenge.

"I'll manage it," I finally said, sliding my hips off the examination table and standing.

It just so happened that Dr. Lane stepped off of the rolling stool at precisely the same time. When I lifted my head, I found her standing barely more than an inch away from me.

Electricity hummed to life at her nearness. She smelled good, a wisp of lavender drifting up to me. Her eyes flicked up to mine, widening slightly. This close, I noticed her gray eyes contained a hint of violet. Her mouth parted slightly when she gasped, drawing my eyes right to her lips. I'd never even noticed her lips before.

Just now, I became acutely aware that they were full and soft. Damn, I wanted to kiss her. She stepped back quickly, her hips bumping into the counter against the wall behind her. The clipboard she'd been holding clattered to the floor.

"Oh shit!" she blurted out as she leaned over to pick it up.

Unfortunately or fortunately, depending on how I looked at it, I leaned down reflexively at the same time. Our hands brushed and a hot jolt zinged through my arm. Her head bumped into my shoulder.

When she straightened, her cheeks were flushed pink. If I thought I'd wanted to kiss her a minute ago, now it was close to irresistible. I shackled the urge.

Meanwhile, the tidy Dr. Lane looked flustered and embarrassed. For the first time, I wasn't annoyed with her. She finally seemed human.

"So you swear," I said with a wink.

Her cheeks flushed a deeper shade of pink. "Obviously I swear," she muttered.

It was almost as if I could see her internally gathering herself back together. She straightened, smoothed a hand over her hair, and then adjusted her glasses. I was starting to get the idea that might be a nervous habit of hers. I'd have given just about anything to see her hair loose.

My words were ahead of my brain. "Do I make you nervous?"

Slick, dude. Because that'll help her relax.

I caught myself about to roll my eyes at my own thoughts.

Dr. Lane looked taken aback by my question. She adjusted her glasses again, looking down at the clipboard I held in my hands. I handed it over to her, and she clutched it tightly to her chest.

"I don't know if nervous is the right word," she finally said. "You seem annoyed whenever you're here, and I'm sorry for that."

Her answer took me off guard. "Oh." For a moment, I almost denied that I'd been annoyed both times I'd been here. But what the hell? It was the truth. Until now that was.

I shrugged. "Sorry about that. It's not your fault. I don't like being injured."

She smiled—and promptly took my breath away.

With her eyes tilting at the corners and the curl of her lips, her sharp features softened. "I don't suppose anyone likes being hurt. Plus, you have a demanding job, and I imagine it's hard for you to take a break."

"That's one way to put it," I answered wryly, shackling my body's out of control response to her. I needed to get out of this small room because her scent was filling my head and making me crazy. Just as I considered what to say to quickly leave, there was a knock at her door.

Chapter Two

CHARLIE

I stared into Jesse Franklin's eyes, little charges of electricity tingling through me from where we'd collided. My cheeks were hot, and I was flustered. But then, every time I saw Jesse Franklin, I was flustered. His gaze held mine—a rich, clear green. I'd never seen a man with eyes like his. With his dark amber hair tousled and wavy, his fit body, and his rugged features—a strong jaw, a prominent nose and angular cheekbones—well, he was unnervingly handsome.

His eyelashes were so thick, they nearly curled to touch his cheeks. It didn't seem quite fair for a man to have eyelashes like that. Nature had been generous to Jesse Franklin in the looks department. His mouth had a sensual curve to it, always making me think completely inappropriate thoughts. He was a patient for God's sake. He'd only been to see me for his shoulder. But still.

I clutched the clipboard to my chest as if it could shield me from the heat dancing through my body. For the first time ever, he didn't seem annoyed with me. As I tried to gather my scattered thoughts into something sensible, there was a knock at the door. Thank God. My body had been frozen in place about an inch from Jesse whose physical presence was so potent, it made me a little crazy.

I stepped back, nearly dropping the clipboard again. Quickly opening the door, I found my medical assistant Rachel there. She smiled, glancing between Jesse and me. "Mrs. Stan is here to see you."

I stared at her, her warm blue gaze unable to calm the anxiety that suddenly swirled inside of me. *Mrs. Stan* was code for a personal issue that had become way too common in my life lately. Worry galloped through my thoughts. I started to hurry out the door, coming to an abrupt stop when Jesse said my name.

"Do I need to make another appointment?" he asked.

Flustered, I turned back to him, adjusting my glasses and trying not to sound too worried. "Of course you do. I'm sorry to rush off. Just a small emergency. Sandy in reception will schedule your next follow up. In the meantime, keep going to see Helen and I'm confident in two weeks, we'll be able to clear you for work."

Jesse held my gaze for a beat, and yet again heat bloomed through me. Under the circumstances, I couldn't believe my body's reaction to him. Lately, my life had been the opposite of inviting for desire or romance. In fact, I'd put those ideas on ice.

As I started hurrying down the hallway, Jesse walked with me, easily keeping pace with his long stride. I was too frazzled to make polite conversation, turning into the door that led to my private office as soon as I reached it.

"I'll see you in two weeks," I said quickly before stepping into my office and closing the door behind me. Leaning against it with a sigh, I took several slow breaths to calm my pulse. I couldn't relax though. I hurried over to my desk, snatching my cell phone off of it and hitting speed dial.

My mother picked up on the first ring. "Where are you? Your father's not home yet, and this doesn't seem like home."

A bite of grief slammed into me. I took a slow breath and swallowed my tears. "Hey, Mom, I'll be home in just a little bit, okay?"

"Where is your father?" she countered, her voice confused.

"He won't be here tonight," I finally said.

I listened as she asked me a few more questions, and I answered with my usual rote answers, trying to keep my tone level and the worry out of my voice. After I hung up, there was a quick knock at my door. "Come in," I called out.

Rachel stepped through the door, closing it behind her. "Everything okay with your mom?"

I looked up into her warm gaze. I wanted to burst into tears, but now definitely wasn't the time. "She's fine. I wish she would remember my dad's dead." My heart thumped another beat of grief.

Rachel's eyes searched my face, but I battened down the hatches inside and took a deep breath. I could handle this. Snagging my coffee mug off my desk, I took a sip of the long cold coffee, the cool bitterness fortifying me.

"Hey, at least Jesse Franklin wasn't too cranky with me today," I said with a chuckle.

Rachel grinned. "I noticed." She paused, cocking her head to the side with a gleam entering her gaze. "I think he likes you."

"Huh?" I asked as I shrugged into my jacket and snatched my purse off of my desk.

"Exactly what I said. He was watching your ass the whole time we walked down the hallway."

A flash of heat scored through me, but I ignored it.

"Um, I think you're crazy. No way was Jesse Franklin checking out my ass."

"Way," Rachel countered with a grin. "He totally was."

"So what? He's my patient and the last thing I have time for is anything related to romance."

Rachel rolled her eyes. "You know Dr. Johnson met his

wife here in the clinic, right? We're almost in the middle of nowhere, and the only thing you've treated Jesse for is a dislocated shoulder. Get over it."

I reached her side, curling my hand around the door-knob. "I have a niece and a mother to take care of, that's my whole life."

Opening the door, I brushed past her. She called out after me. "Yeah, well maybe it would be good to expand your horizons."

I didn't reply because I couldn't. I didn't want to be rude, but I needed to go, or the tears pressing hot at the backs of my eyes and the emotion tightening my throat would let loose. Hurrying down the hallway, I mentally ran through what I needed to pick up at the grocery store before racing home as fast as possible.

Jesse Franklin, whether or not he had been staring at my ass, wasn't a man I could consider. I barely had time for fantasies. Not to mention, if he knew anything about my crazy life, he'd run far and fast in the opposite direction. Any sane man would.

Chapter Three

JESSE

A week had passed since my last appointment with the delectable Dr. Lane. Damn. She'd kept my thoughts occupied to say the least. Just a few seconds of her guard down and she'd set me on fire. I was oddly looking forward to my next appointment with her. I was still impatient to be cleared for work because I was bored out of my fucking mind.

Meanwhile, that afternoon my dog was pacing by the windows, whining and occasionally barking, her gaze focused on the trees to the side of my house. Waffle was a mutt, although the vet was pretty confident she was mostly some kind of hound. She had floppy ears and silky fur with black and gold markings. The last time she'd been like this, I'd discovered a few hikers on the back of my property. I didn't mind the live and let live lifestyle in Alaska, but I wasn't cool with people walking on my property without my permission.

With Waffle at my side, I headed out into the trees through the melting, patchy snow. I knew I wouldn't have to look too long because she'd lead me straight to whatever, or whoever, had her worked up. A few minutes later, I reached the back corner of my property. I watched Waffle sniff along a set of footprints following a trail that ran from my property to the adjoining property.

Puzzled, I followed her, eyeing the meandering path of footprints. They weren't what I expected. I'd have expected hiking boot treads and most likely larger. These footprints were small and barely much larger than the size of my own hand. They were small enough, I even wondered if it was a kid just wandering around. Within a few minutes, the sound of Waffle bounding through the trees slowed.

Magpies chattered in the forest around me and nearby squirrels made all kinds of racket, clearly offended by our presence here. Glancing up, my mouth dropped open. An elderly woman garbed in a flowing skirt and blouse was looking down at Waffle and stroking a hand down her back. She stood on a small rise, looking out over a valley in the distance.

This part of Alaska was a mix of mostly spruce forest mingled with birch and cottonwood. Willow Brook was in the foothills of the Alaska Range, offering small valleys and openings amongst the trees. This section of land belonged to Claire Parker, who had moved out of state years back and rented the home on her property. I didn't know who was renting it at the moment.

I approached the woman, completely puzzled as to what she was doing out here. She most certainly wasn't dressed for the weather. It was early spring, technically, which didn't mean much. There was still snow on the ground and winter held the air in its teeth, the sharp bite of cold still strong. A skirt and blouse would be no match against hypothermia if she were out here for long. She was engrossed in petting Waffle, talking to her softly.

"Hello?" I called as I approached.

She turned, a gentle smile breaking across her face. "Hello," she replied as if it was perfectly normal to be standing in the woods this time of year wearing sneakers, but otherwise dressed as if she were going out for dinner. Her face was lined and weathered. She was quite lovely with long black hair shot through with silver, held back with a barrette on the top of her head. Her eyes were wide and gray with a hint of violet to them. She reminded me of someone, but I couldn't put my finger on who.

"I'm looking for Danny," she said as if I should know who that was.

I wasn't familiar with anyone named Danny. She looked befuddled and was clearly oblivious to the fact that if she were out here for too long, she would easily get hypothermia. I decided to just be as friendly and walk her back to my place to take her down to the hospital. Calling the station at this point wouldn't get her there any quicker. We had a good half-mile walk to my house.

"Well, I'm not sure where Danny is, but my name is Jesse. Why don't you come with me and then maybe I can help you find him?"

She seemed to like that idea, smiling brightly. "Okay," she said with another stroke along Waffle's back. She walked at my side as we headed back through the woods. Waffle seemed as concerned about her as I was, sticking close to her side as we trudged slowly through the melting snow. Shrugging out of my jacket, I draped it over her shoulders when I saw the fine shiver running through her.

"I don't think I've met you before," I said conversationally.

"Oh no?" she replied, as if puzzled by this. "I'm from here. Just down the road. Charlie, Emily, Danny and me."

"I didn't catch your name," I replied, hoping she'd offer it up.

She stumbled slightly when her foot caught on a root, and I steadied her with a hand.

"Oh, I'm Olive. Do you know Charlie?"

"You know, I'm not sure I do," I offered, running through the various Charlies I knew locally.

Despite the rest of Olive's outfit not making a lick of sense for this weather, she had on good walking shoes. They wouldn't keep the moisture out and certainly wouldn't have kept her warm if she'd stayed out much longer, but they were perfectly fine for walking. In short order, we reached my place. Once we were in my truck, I called our station dispatcher, Maisie, to let her know I was bringing Olive to the hospital. I was concerned about her and fairly certain she was completely lost.

As soon as I explained, Maisie sighed. "Oh thank God. I didn't even know you were on duty."

"I'm not, but Waffle was barking and pacing, so I took her out. We found her at the back corner of my property. What's up?"

Maisie started to reply, but then got another call. "Gotta go. I'll call when I can."

We arrived at the hospital, and Holly Blake was the nurse who met us at the ER. For that, I was relieved. I'd known Holly for a few years, and she was steady as a rock. Her blond hair was tied up in a slapdash ponytail and her brown eyes crinkled at the corners with her smile when she saw me. She seemed to recognize Olive. Before I had a chance to ask questions, she led us to an examination room and situated Olive in a chair.

"I'll call Charlie in just a minute," she said to Olive. Catching my eyes, she nudged her head to the side, indicating we should step out.

Once we were in the hallway, she started to speak, but we were cut off by Dr. Lane, her eyes wide and her cheeks flushed. She came hurrying down the hall, skidding to a stop in front of us. "Please tell me she's okay."

Holly nodded quickly. "She's fine, Charlie. Go on in," she said, gesturing to the door.

The pieces started to fall into place. This was the *Charlie* that Olive was talking about. What the hell was going on?

Dr. Lane, as I knew her, didn't even bother to say hello,

her eyes flicking to me and then away as she hurried into the room.

"Who is that?" I asked Holly as soon as Dr. Lane closed the door behind her.

"That's Charlie's mother. She has dementia, and she gets lost sometimes."

As I stared at Holly, absorbing the implications, a sad look crossed her face. "I can't believe what that must be like. Lately, it's been happening more. Where did you find her?"

"Waffle was restless, whining, and barking, so I thought there were some hikers on my property. I headed out to the back corner to check, and we found her instead. She was asking where Danny was."

Holly nodded as if all of this made perfect sense. "Yeah, they live right next door to you in Claire's old place. Danny is Olive's late husband, but she forgets he passed away a few years ago. Anyway, we're so glad you found her."

Holly's pager went off. "Gotta go. If Charlie comes out, tell her another nurse will be here in a sec." She hurried off, giving me a little wave. Another nurse approached and stepped into the room.

This would normally be the cue for me to go. I had no reason to hang around at this point. Yet, I didn't quite feel right about leaving just yet. The nurse came out another moment later with Olive in a wheelchair. Olive smiled brightly at me, waving as she passed by. The nurse flashed a distracted smile as she spoke to Olive. "We're just gonna check on a few things."

I stood there in the hallway, wondering if Dr. Lane was okay. I'd just about talked myself into leaving when I heard the sound of sobbing. I knocked lightly on the door and stepped in without even pausing to think. Dr. Lane was leaning against the examination table in the center of the room, her hands over her face as she took a shuddering breath.

She didn't appear to have heard me knocking, or stepping into the room. "Are you okay?"

Her breath stuttered, and she lifted her head. Her gray eyes were wide, her cheeks flushed and damp from her tears. She swiped at them with her thumb, collecting herself quickly. "Thank you for finding her. She's been gone for over an hour, and I've been so worried."

"It was kind of by accident. I'm not even on duty, so I didn't know you'd put a call in. She wandered close to the back of my property earlier. My dog was pacing and whining. Honestly, I thought she was a hiker on my property without permission, so I walked out there to check. That's how I found her. I'd like to take credit, but you should thank Waffle, not me."

"Waffle?" she asked, a smile barely teasing the corners of her lips.

I really wanted her to smile. I didn't like seeing her like this. The Dr. Lane I knew, all two times I'd met her, was put together and sharp. My heart twisted to see her look so concerned.

"My dog," I explained.

I stood there, my hands stuffed in my pockets as I fought the urge to pull her into my arms. Because she looked sad and worried, nothing like the buttoned up, proper doctor I was used to seeing. Right now, she didn't have on her lab coat. She had on a pair of leggings and a fitted T-shirt. Her hair, usually pulled back tightly, had fallen loose as if she'd run her hands through it a few too many times. It fell in a tousle around her shoulders, that streak of purple I'd noticed before standing out amidst the glossy brown locks.

Even though it was completely nonsensical given the setting, my body had some thoughts about how she looked. Her T-shirt was pulled tight across her breasts. Garbed in her lab coat at her office, I wouldn't have guessed she had curves like this. But damn, she had curves for days.

With a hard mental shake, I knocked that train of thought off its tracks.

"Dr. Lane..." I started to say.

She shook her head. "No need to call me that, just call me Charlie. That's what everyone else calls me anyway."

"Ah, so it took me finding your lost mom to get that privilege?" I asked with a careful smile.

She rolled her eyes. "No, it wasn't that. You were just too cranky with me, so I never got around to it. Neil always says he never goes by Dr. Johnson because the town's too small."

"True, some of us call him Doc, but the rest of us call him Neil. I'm sorry about your mom. Next time she goes missing, just give me a call first because I'm close by. Well, more like a quarter-mile down the road, but still. Waffle can help find her pretty quick. I'm not saying don't call 9-1-1, I'm just saying it's easy for me to help look for her."

Charlie nodded, dragging her sleeve across her face. "I need to find someone to watch her during the day, but she gets upset every time I bring it up."

"She mentioned that she lived here for years, but that doesn't seem right. I mean, you just moved here a bit ago, right?"

Charlie lips curled in a tired smile. "My parents lived here a long time ago. Actually, I was born close to here. My dad was stationed at Elmendorf Air Force Base, just outside of Anchorage. He later got stationed elsewhere, but they always missed Alaska and meant to move back here. You know how it goes though. They meant to do it, but it never happened. After my dad died, I thought maybe she'd like it because she talked about it so much."

"That makes sense," I replied.

Charlie's shoulders rose and fell with a shuddering breath. Her gaze broke from mine, and she turned to snag a tissue off the counter nearby, blowing her nose quickly and then grabbing another one to dab at her eyes.

"You must think I'm an idiot," she muttered. "Crying, moving here just because my mom missed it."

"Not at all," I said, meaning it completely. "Why would you think that?"

"Well, when we got here, my mom wasn't as bad as she is now. But she's gone downhill fast. I didn't really think about what it meant to get a house in the woods where she could wander off. It would be better if we were somewhere where there were more people around."

I stared at her for a moment, unsure what to say, but then I figured I might as well be honest. "I don't know. If you were in a busy area, she could wander off and just get lost in the city. At least here, once everybody gets to know her, people will keep an eye out for her. Plus, now that I know you're my neighbor, I can check on her when I'm around. It's not a big deal. I'll bring Waffle over to visit her too."

Charlie stared at me, and then burst out laughing. Tears were rolling down her cheeks again by the time she stopped. Again, I found myself resisting the urge to pull her into my arms. "What's so funny?"

She gulped in air and then shrugged. "Having your dog visit her. I dunno. It seemed funny."

"I suppose, but if it weren't for Waffle, I might not have found her today. If she gets to know your mom, she'll find her easy every time. She's a hound mix, and let me tell you, she follows her nose."

Charlie's gray eyes scanned my face, a small smile teasing her lips. "I guess that makes sense then."

We stared at each other, the room getting quiet. I didn't know what else to say. Her mother was fine, and I should leave. There was no reason for me to linger. Yet, I found myself wanting to stay. Actually, what I wanted to do was kiss her. But that was totally out of place and half-crazy, and I damn well knew it.

I started to turn just as Charlie moved. The room was

small. Her phone rang. She slipped her phone out of her pocket, glancing at the screen. "I have to take this if you don't mind."

"Sure, of course. I'll just..."

"No, don't go," she said.

Without even thinking about it, I simply nodded and waited.

"Hey, Emily, what is it?"

Charlie listened and then nodded. "I'm with grandma at the hospital right now. We'll be home in a little bit. I can pick up pizza on the way home."

Whatever Emily's reply was, it didn't seem too friendly with Charlie's brow furrowing and her hand gripping the phone tightly as she spoke. My curiosity about her was piling up. Nothing about her was fitting in with what I had expected. But then, I didn't know what I'd expected.

After Charlie hung up the phone, her eyes caught mine. "My niece. She lives with us too. She's fifteen years old, and she kind of hates me some days," she offered with a sigh.

Warning bells should have been going off in my mind. Hell, she had a mother who seemed to be on the way to senile and apparently a teenage niece who hated her. I didn't know what the hell I was thinking. Except I couldn't stop looking at her. Her gorgeous gray eyes, that whimsical purple streak in her hair. To see her out of her usual lab coat and buttoned up look, well fuck me. She still had her glasses on, but her tousled hair softened her features.

As she looked at me, the air started to heat, and my body tightened. I didn't know what it was about her. I heard nothing and thought nothing. My entire focus narrowed to her—to the fine arch of her brows, the angle of her cheekbones, and her full lips, which seemed out of place in her otherwise sharp-featured face.

Her wide gray eyes stared back at me, darkening like the summer sky on a stormy day. The air hummed. Before I thought about it—but let's face it, I wasn't really thinking, not with my brain—I stepped in her direction. At the same time, she took a step, bringing us flush together. Lifting a hand, I slid my fingers through her hair, the locks silky soft. I could see her pulse fluttering in her neck. Her cheeks flushed pink, her lips parted, and the next thing I knew, I was threading my hand into her hair.

Cupping the nape of her neck, I dipped my head and dusted a kiss over her lips. A small sound came from her throat, something between a hum and a moan. Coming from her, it was like spurs to my need. I swiped my tongue along the seam of her lips. Her mouth opened on a gasp. She tasted divine—sweet with a hint of mint, her mouth warm and welcoming. The uptight Dr. Lane, excuse me Charlie, moaned into my mouth.

Fuck me. She kissed like a dream, her tongue tangling sensually with mine, her hand sliding up to grip my hair. I lost sight of everything but the feel of her against me, her mouth moving under mine and those luscious curves that I hadn't known existed pressed against me.

A sharp knock at the door punctured the haze in my mind. I broke free, looking down into her gray eyes, dark and flashing silver.

"Oh," she said, her eyes widening. Yet, she didn't move and I didn't want her to move.

Chapter Four

CHARLIE

Staring up into Jesse's eyes, I tried to catch my breath. I tried to think. But thought was hard to come by. All I could focus on was the feel of him against me.

The man might as well have been sculpted from stone, all coiled muscle and power. Just now, every inch of him was pressed against me. Somewhere in the middle of the madness of our kiss, his hand had slid down my spine to cup my bottom. I felt as if I were falling with butterflies spinning wildly in my core.

Desire throbbed inside, sending heat and liquid need sliding through my veins. Another sharp knock at the door nudged me, mentally kicking through the haze and madness in my mind.

"Oh!"

I forced myself to jump back. Because, let me tell you, my body did *not* want to move. I could've stood there for days with the feel of Jesse pressed against me. It wasn't simply desire, it was feeling encompassed by his strength. Oh, and I might mention the man kissed like a dream—soft and masterful. I nearly melted the moment his lips met mine and his hand threaded in my hair.

It was an act of will to step further away from him. My body was drawn so powerfully to his, like magnet to metal. Jesse's eyes stayed on mine, making me feel as if he could see right through me. Yet, when I met his gaze, I didn't feel the judgment I expected to see.

Oh no. It was something else altogether. The heat in his gaze seared me, and something else flickered underneath. My belly fluttered and my heart clenched.

I gave myself a mental shake, turning to answer the door. It was Holly Blake, a nurse who I'd come to really like. I imagined I could be friends with her, but my life didn't leave much room for friends, not lately.

"How is she?" I asked.

Holly leaned against the doorframe, glancing between us with a smile. "She's fine. She's up front talking to Penny. You know she loves her."

Relief washed over me. "I know she does. Thank you, Holly. I guess I'll get going."

Holly looked over to Jesse. "We're glad you found Olive."

Jesse shrugged. "Just luck this time. Now that I know she's next door, I'll pay better attention when I'm around. Plus, I'm going to bring Waffle over to meet her."

Holly grinned and winked just as her pager went off. "Gotta run. See you soon," she said with a quick wave before hurrying off.

Uncertain what to say, I looked over to Jesse. I didn't quite know the playbook for conversation after I'd been at the end of my tether and my too-handsome, too-sexy neighbor found my mother wandering in the woods and then I kissed him.

He saved me.

"I'll bring Waffle by this evening. If you'd like, I'll pick up the pizza. I'm guessing you'd like to get your mother home sooner rather than later. No need to make an extra stop."

I stared at him, wondering why he was being so nice. But then I reminded myself I didn't need to be suspicious. If there was one thing I had learned in the six months or so that I'd been in Willow Brook was the people were nice here. Not the superficial, polite nice, but the down-to-earth-pull-your-car-out-of-a-ditch-in-any-weather kind of nice.

"That would be great. Emily will want vegetarian something, but my mom likes pepperoni. I'll pay you back."

"No need," he replied easily. "I can handle two pizzas. Come on, I'll walk you out."

He held the door as we turned, his hand brushing on my back as I stepped past him. The casual touch sent sparks skittering through my body, which I willed myself to ignore.

When we got to the front desk, my mom was standing there talking with the receptionist. They were discussing gardening, something my mother loved. I was looking forward to this coming summer on her behalf. She'd spent hours poring over gardening catalogs, something she'd done for as long as I could remember. I hoped it would give her something to focus on. She smiled at me, her eyes moving past me to Jesse almost immediately. She appeared to recognize him.

"Hi, Olive, how we doing?" he asked, his manner easygoing.

"Are you driving us home?" she asked.

"Mom, I'm driving."

She glanced to me as if she'd forgotten I was there. "But I like Jesse."

He grinned. "Well, you're going to see me in a little bit. I'll stop by with pizza."

My mom smiled widely, delighted at the prospect. "Perfect, pepperoni please," she said.

If I hadn't known the events of the day, I'd have assumed she'd known Jesse for longer than this afternoon. I didn't even know what to think, but I was getting accustomed to the whims of her memory. I was a doctor, and I understood how senility and dementia unfolded differently for everyone. Yet, it was difficult for me to see clearly with my mother. I loved her, and it was painful to witness her slow slide. It was strange to adjust to the reversal in our roles—where I needed to take care of her rather than the other way around.

Jesse nodded. "I'll see you soon."

As he left, my mom turned to me. "I have to pee," she announced.

As if by magic, another nurse who knew my mother happened to be walking by. "Come on. I'll take you. It's right over here," she said with a warm smile in my direction.

I breathed a silent sigh of relief. Not that I minded taking my mother to the restroom, but I needed to make sure the insurance details were taken care of. After my mother walked away, Penny, the friendly receptionist smiled at me. "Your mom is a sweetheart. I asked Holly to send over a list of care attendants for you. I know you want to do it all yourself, but a little help never hurt anyone."

I met Penny's eyes and tried to smile, my heart giving a sad squeeze. Because my mom was great, and I loved her dearly. "She likes talking to you, so thanks for always being so nice."

"No need to thank me for talking. If you ask my daughter, I talk too damned much," she offered with a chuckle. Pausing, she cocked her head to the side.

Sensing where she was going, I said, "I know it would help to arrange for someone to help out when I'm at work, but every time I bring it up, my mom gets upset. I promise, I'm not being stubborn."

Penny nodded slowly. "I understand, but I promise, I only put the ones I thought your mother might like on that list. If that helps." Tapping on her keyboard, she confirmed my mother's insurance information. Her gaze bounced to the doorway where Jesse had paused to speak to someone.

"Jesse's a good guy. He'll keep an eye out for her when he's home. Plus, he's got Waffle who wants to smell the whole wide world."

I couldn't help but laugh at that. "You know Waffle?"

Penny grinned. "Course I do. Jesse's mom's a good friend of mine."

My phone buzzed, and I glanced at it to see a text from Emily asking when we'd be home. A sense of weariness held tight inside—two people shouldn't be too many to take care of, but when I felt as if I were stumbling every step of the way, sometimes it did.

"Time to get going," I said, flashing a smile at Penny. "Thanks again, and I promise I'll follow up on getting some help."

Chapter Five

CHARLIE

In short order, I was back at the house getting Mom settled at the kitchen table and then going to knock on my niece's door. "Em?" I called.

Silence greeted me. I knocked again, calling her name once more. Nothing. I opened the door to find her on her bed, staring at her computer with her headphones on. She hadn't even noticed that I'd opened the door. I took a deep breath, letting it out in a slow sigh. For a moment, I just looked at her. She looked so much like my sister it was startling sometimes.

With her glossy dark hair and her wide gray eyes, she was lovely. Unlike my late sister and myself, Emily kept her hair cut short. It stood up in spiky tufts. Her bright purple glasses sat low on her nose. With her knees tucked up, she looked so young. She had a buzzy energy, even when she was sitting still. I could practically feel the wheels spinning in her brain from here.

I waited to see if she was going to notice me. When she didn't, I walked in and sat on the foot of the bed. She finally looked up when the bed moved with my weight sinking onto the mattress. With a gentle tug, her ear buds fell out, and she looked up at me, pushing her glasses up on her nose. "What?"

"Hi, Em, it's nice to see you too," I offered with a slight smile.

Em smiled back, but just barely. Her gaze was sullen and guarded. I often felt as if she were waiting for me to annoy her.

"Hi, Aunt Charlie. Do you have pizza?"

I opted to ignore that question for now. "Grandma is fine, if you were wondering."

Her cheeks flushed, and she moved her laptop to the side, folding her knees out.

"Oh good, I'm sorry. I should've asked right away. When I came home and she wasn't here, well that's when I called you. You know I could've gone to look for her," she said, her gaze earnest.

"I know. But then if she came home and you weren't here, we wouldn't know. I figured it was best if you waited here."

"Who found her?"

"Actually, our neighbor. He brought her to the hospital."

"We have neighbors?" she asked with a roll of her eyes.

Emily wasn't having the best adjustment to our new life outside of the city. I'd moved here for more than one reason. Just as I'd told Jesse, I'd been born nearby and my mom had always missed Alaska. That had been the genesis of the idea.

But Emily had also gotten into a bit of trouble in Boston. Her mother, my sister, had died of cancer last year only six months after my father passed away. It had been a rough year for all of us. Somewhere in the midst of that, Emily had gotten mixed up with the wrong crowd in high school.

She was too damned smart for her own good, but she'd been vulnerable, sad, missing her mother, and seeking attention the way most kids did at her age. I'd thought a fresh start for all of us would be good. But Emily wasn't loving much of anything. Her one soft spot was my mom.

"Of course we have neighbors. Jesse lives just down the road. His dog started barking, so he went to check the back of his property and found Gram. He brought her to the hospital, and they called me. He's bringing the pizza and his dog over in a bit."

Emily's eyes widened and a smile followed. "Really?"

A genuine smile from her was such a welcome sight, I wanted to hug her.

"He has a dog?"

"Yup. Come on, let's go downstairs."

In a rare moment, she didn't sulk and followed me downstairs. She gave her grandma a kiss and then sat down to play cards with her. I thanked the stars for the millionth time that Em enjoyed playing cards. My mom loved it, and it was something they could do together.

Meanwhile, I took a look at the kitchen sink, which was filled with dishes. I could've scolded Em for not cleaning up, but I wasn't up for it today. I was rinsing my hands after loading the dishwasher when there was a knock at the door.

"Can you get that, Em?" I called over my shoulder, figuring it was Jesse.

The moment I heard his voice, heat rolled through me, the memory of our kiss flashing in my thoughts. I'd kind of blocked it out. Between driving home with my mom and feeling emotionally exhausted from the afternoon, I hadn't wanted to think about it. Because it was insane.

Kissing anyone wasn't something I had time for. At all. Much less the ramifications of kissing someone who was my patient. Layered on top of that, I had a mother with dementia to take care of and a niece who was grieving her own mother. I was still dealing with my own grief between my sister and my father dying inside of a year.

Kissing anyone, or contemplating romance at all, was *way* at the bottom of my priority list. So far down, I didn't think it even rated being on a list. Yet, that didn't change how my body reacted to Jesse. God, that man could kiss.

As soon as I heard the door open and close, I turned off the water and gave my hands a shake. Drying my hands, I turned to see Jesse entering with three pizza boxes and a dog. The dog loped into the living room, immediately making a beeline for Emily and flinging herself at her feet. Em squealed and leaned over to pet the dog.

I caught Jesse's eyes, from across the room, and my belly spun, a flash of heat zinging through me. With his green gaze holding mine, it felt as if there was a band of electricity humming between us across the room.

"Hello, hello," Jesse said. "Where should I put this?"

Emily was so focused on his dog, I didn't even bother to prompt her to greet him. "Over here," I said, gesturing to the kitchen counter.

He strolled across the room, passing my mother at the table. "Hello, Olive," he said with a smile.

She looked up from studying her cards, her eyes cloudy for a moment before her expression cleared. "Oh hi. So good to see you again."

"Same to you." He reached the counter and set the pizza boxes down.

I spoke quietly, "If she forgets your name, don't take it personally."

"I wouldn't, but thanks for the heads up. How's she doing?"

"She's fine. You'd never know she wandered off for an hour today. I think this is harder on me than her. Let me introduce you to my niece. She's so excited to meet your dog."

I turned, glancing back to gesture for him to follow me back into the living room The home was two stories with the three bedrooms upstairs. The downstairs was open with the living room and kitchen together, and a bathroom and laundry in the back.

Pausing in front of Emily where she was on the floor petting Jesse's dog, I smiled down at her. "Anything you forgot to say?"

Jesse's dog was slender with black and gold fur and big floppy years.

Emily looked up with a grin. "Hi, I'm Emily."

Jesse nodded. "And I'm Jesse. That's Waffle," he said pointing toward the dog.

Emily threw her arms around Waffle, hugging her close. "I'm so glad you brought her over. I didn't even know we had neighbors nearby."

Jesse grinned and a prickle ran down my spine. Again. God why did he have to affect me so easily? It was easier when he was rude to me. Don't get me wrong, it wasn't like I hadn't noticed how handsome he was. You'd have to be blind not to notice. With his amber hair, green eyes, and rugged body, he was all kinds of man.

"Yup. You have neighbors. More than me too. Claire's been renting this property out for years. How long have you been here?" he asked, looking my way when it was obvious Emily could only focus on Waffle.

"Just about six months. We started somewhere else first, but that was a seasonal rental."

Jesse nodded. "Yeah, lots of those around here."

"Do you want some pizza?" I asked, looking back to Emily.

That got her off the floor. With a quick nod, she hurried across the room to the kitchen. Glancing up at Jesse, I wished my body would behave. He'd made me antsy before, if only because he'd been so cranky. Yet, Jesse nice — well, that was something else altogether.

Given the choice, I probably preferred cranky. Likely because I felt like I had some semblance of control. Now, when I met his rich green gaze, my belly flipped and a wash of heat rolled through me. I instantly recalled the feel of his lips on mine.

Emily said something to Waffle as she carried her plate to the couch, effectively snapping me back to sanity.

"Come on, we'll go ahead and sit down. I know you brought Waffle over for my mom, but it's put Em in a good mood so that's a win."

Jesse's slow chuckle sent a shiver over the surface of my skin. Ignoring it, I spun away and walked toward the kitchen counter. I'd loved this house the moment I saw it. The space was open and airy. The kitchen was to the back with windows looking into the trees. A counter running against the back wall had a sink centered in front of the windows and a built-in wall oven on one side. There was an island opposite the counter with a stovetop in the center of it, offering an easy way to work in the kitchen.

The dining room table was off to the side where my mother sat right now, flipping through a magazine. She'd already lost track of Jesse's presence. The living room was just beyond with the soft gray tile from the kitchen floor transitioning to hardwood flooring through the living room and the remainder of the house.

The home had come furnished with a sectional couch, a large, comfy ottoman, a flat screen TV mounted on the wall, and built-in bookshelves on either side of the living room area. There were windows floor to ceiling on either side with a side door that led onto the deck. The windows offered a beautiful view of the mountains in the distance.

Moving here had helped me understand why my parents had loved Alaska so much. My memories from my time here were vague as we'd moved away when I was five-years old. The experience of being this close to the wilderness was grounding in a way. The views were, of course, stunning. It felt as if we were living in a postcard some days.

Jesse followed me to the counter, glancing over to my mother where she sat at the table. "I'm assuming we'll eat at the table," he commented.

Catching his eyes and willing my pulse to slow, I nodded.

"Plates are right there. Would you like something to drink? We have beer, wine, juice, and water."

"A beer sounds great. I walked over from my place with Waffle. Figured it would be a good evening walk for her."

I wasn't quite sure where he lived. I knew he mentioned he lived nearby, but nearby didn't mean I could see the house. "Where's your place?" I asked as I fetched him a beer from the refrigerator.

As he slid two pieces of pepperoni pizza onto a plate, he nodded toward the back deck. "To the right. Just east of here. The Bakers own the house on the other side. They're snowbirds," he explained.

"Snowbirds?" I asked as I got a plate ready for my mother and myself.

He chuckled as he turned away, walking to the dining table. "Snowbirds are people who fly away for the winter."

He slipped into a chair at an angle across from my mother, glancing over when she looked up. "Hi, Olive," he offered with a nod before he took a swallow of his beer.

My mother smiled. For a moment, her gaze was blank and then she appeared to recognize him again. "Jesse."

"You got it," he said easily.

I realized that in his job, he likely often interacted with all kinds of people, but I still appreciated how easy he was with my mother. He didn't seem to expect much from her, yet he was friendly and comfortable when she clicked into gear to talk.

I set my mother's plate down in front of her, handing her a napkin and a glass of water. As I poured a glass of wine for myself, I called over to Emily.

I tried not to be too picky with rules, but I did try to make sure we actually had a meal together every night. She ignored me for a moment, but Jesse let out a low whistle and Waffle scrambled up from the floor to hurry over.

Whether he did that to help me or not, I didn't know. But it helped. Em glanced over her shoulder and then snagged her plate from the coffee table to join us. Waffle settled on the floor by my mother's feet. She seemed to be a sweet dog. Meanwhile, Em slipped into the chair beside my mother.

Dinner went smoothly for the first time in weeks. I had no doubt the presence of Waffle was the key factor. Em would've had no problem being rude to Jessie. She didn't discriminate with her attitude. But she adored dogs, so her mood overall was better. I didn't quite know what to think of this impromptu dinner, but I wasn't going to complain. Willow Brook was a small town, and it had already become evident that people tended to take care of each other around here. I just hadn't had a chance to get to know any of my neighbors. It might've been slightly disconcerting that I'd had a random, hot-as-hell kiss with this particular neighbor. But I thought I did a fabulous job of mostly ignoring that detail.

Later that night, after Jesse insisted on helping me load the dishwasher and Em had gone up to her room, I looked over to see my mother asleep in her chair at the table.

"Thank you," I said, glancing up and catching Jessie's eyes. He turned, leaning his hips against the counter with one hand hooked in the pocket of his jeans. Sweet hell. All that man had to do was exist, and he was sexy.

I tried to kick the thoughts away, but my pulse didn't listen, speeding up again when his eyes caught mine. "No problem. Waffle's a sweetheart. She found your mom before she knew her this time, so if your mom wanders off again, just give me a call. I'm not always around, but if I am, I'm happy to help."

Emotion abruptly welled inside, tears pressing at the backs of my eyes. The ridiculousness of my life hit me every so often. I felt so alone most of the time. Lately, I felt completely out of sorts. By nature, I was a cheerful person. But cheer was hard to come by these days. The weight of trying to come to terms with my mother's slow slide into dementia was more painful than I could have imagined. Layered onto that everything I'd been through with my family in the last few years, and Jesse's simple offer meant more than he could imagine, and I didn't quite know how to take it.

I planned to take Penny's warm, but pointed advice that I needed to find some help during the days for my mother. Yet, just the thought that there was someone to call lifted a weight from me. However, the last thing I wanted was to start crying in front of him. Again. Because that would be ridiculous. He'd already found me crying once.

So I swallowed through the emotion clogging my throat, hoping my tears didn't show in my eyes. "Thank you. It helps now that I'm starting to get to know a few people around town. Penny's given me some suggestions of people who could come watch her during the day, and I'm going to look into that. Emily's great at helping out after school, but I don't like her being responsible for it. It's too much. She's only fifteen."

Jesse nodded slowly. "Maybe so. But she seems to have a lot of patience for her grandmother. As teenagers go, she could be a lot less friendly about it," he said with a little chuckle.

"You familiar with teenagers?"

Jesse's eyes crinkled at the corners with his smile. "Oh yeah. My brother has a daughter who's fifteen too. Wouldn't be surprised if they're in the same grade together. Anyway, let's just say she might not have as much patience with our mother as Emily does with yours. She's a good kid, but she's got other things on her mind. Usually it's her latest boyfriend."

I had to bite my lip to keep from begging him to let me introduce Em to his niece. She'd been grumping about making friends here ever since we moved. She was a sweet kid, but she had withdrawn ever since her mom died. Back in Boston, she'd had a small circle of friends, but she'd never been the most outgoing girl. Her mom's death had hit her hard, and she'd withdrawn even further. In the midst of the aftermath, she'd started dating a boy who was dabbling in drugs and subsequently got expelled from school for having drugs on school grounds. Though I didn't believe Em had gotten tangled up in that, it had shown me how vulnerable she was to sliding into the wrong crowd.

Another downside I hadn't considered moving to Willow Brook was how it might feel for a teenager to start over in a small community like this. But then I hadn't been thinking clearly for too damned long.

I shut my mind off of the what if's. No sense in rehashing a decision that had already been made. I met Jesse's smile with one of my own.

"I know. She's good with her. Em's not the most typical teen these days. Except when she's annoyed with me, that is."

Jesse winked and chuckled, turning when my mother said his name. I forced myself to look away as he stepped over to her, responding to whatever she said.

It was late enough, I needed to get to bed and make sure my mom was settled for the night. Jesse said his goodbyes, and I watched from the windows as he disappeared into the trees with Waffle jogging at his sides.

Chapter Six

CHARLIE

Later that night, I lay in bed staring at the ceiling. Whoever had rented this home before us had left constellations on the ceiling with glow in the dark paint. Every night, I looked up at a replica of the starlit sky outside the windows. Smack in the middle of the constellations was a skylight where you could see the Little Dipper. Whoever had painted the ceiling had an eye for detail. After I figured out what they'd done, I'd taken a picture one night in the darkness and compared it to the stars outside. They'd recreated the entire sky around the constellation showing through the skylight.

I wondered if Jesse would know who had painted it. The moment my thoughts spun to him, heat bloomed through me. I couldn't shake the memory of the way his lips felt against mine. I'd have thought a rather mundane dinner with my mother asking the same questions over and over, conversation repeated on a loop, would've snuffed out any desire flickering between Jesse and I.

But no. Oh no.

It wasn't as if I'd been lusting after Jesse during dinner. Not at all. It was simply that watching him with my mother

and with Emily and his sweet dog Waffle had only complicated matters. He wasn't the man I'd expected. At all.

Before I'd known him as a rather irritable, sexy-as-hell
hotshot firefighter. Now I also knew him to be a rather kind,
funny man. Sleep was hard to come by. My mind kept
flashing back to his tongue swiping across my lips and
delving inside. I shifted my legs restlessly, the moisture
between my thighs shocking me. Fantasy had been far from
my thoughts. But right now, there was no sleep to be had,
not with Jesse hot on my brain, and my body humming with
need.

I could feel my nipples puckering against my thin T-
shirt, and I finally gave in, sliding my hand between my
thighs into the slick, wet heat there. In a matter of seconds,
my channel clenched around my fingers and sparks of pleasure scattered through me.

I finally fell asleep, only to wake the following morning
with Jesse dancing through my thoughts. Making a decision
that morning as soon as I got to the office, I told Sandy to
switch Jesse over to Dr. Johnson and not to schedule any
further appointments for him with me. I didn't care that it
was a small town, and that I'd only seen him for nothing
more than a dislocated shoulder. It didn't feel right to climax
on my own hand with thoughts of him, knowing that I
might see him again as a patient.

Sandy looked askance at me, but she did as I asked. Just
when I knew she was going to ask why, the office phone
rang. Saved by the phone, I hurried off.

Later, after a very busy day, I sank into the chair in my
office with a sigh. Closing my eyes, I leaned my head back
for a few moments. When I'd gone to medical school, I had
originally intended to specialize in something. Yet, my father
passed away from complications from a stroke and my sister
died after a battle with pancreatic cancer.

My reserves had been deleted, and I hadn't had it in me
to take more than the three years of residency required for

family medicine. Between my mother's grief, my own, and Emily's, my last year of residency had been challenging. That didn't even take into account the two years before that after my sister's diagnosis. I'd been so muddled, the idea of moving to Alaska had seemed like a lifeline.

By accident, I'd discovered my default choice of family medicine was the best choice for me. I was never bored, and the variety in my daily work made it fun. Take today. My day had started seeing an elderly woman for a cough that she couldn't shake before I'd moved on to a harried mother who got a paperclip stuck in her thigh when her toddler accidentally stabbed her with it. She'd laughed with me about it. There were a few others in the mix, and then my day ended with a cheerful little boy who had broken his big toe when he thought he could kick the stairs away.

It was just his toe, but a broken big toe could be painful. He'd been quite the good sport about it. His mother had simply laughed and shaken her head.

Aside from the various stressors that came with moving to Alaska, I was growing to love it here — the way everybody treated me as if I would become a friend even if I wasn't yet, the way I felt as I was getting to know the town itself the more time I spent here.

Opening my eyes, I spun in my chair to look out the windows. You couldn't beat the view here. Dr. Johnson's office was in downtown Willow Brook. The term downtown here was quite different from downtown Boston, or say, any other city. His office was on a side street off of Main Street. Like much of downtown, it offered a view of Swan Lake. Swan Lake was smack in the middle of Willow Brook. It was a large, sprawling lake with lodges circling most of it and wilderness on the far side.

With it being early spring, the days were getting longer. I was finding the shift from winter into spring here interesting. I was accustomed to winter. Boston certainly had its share of winter, but the darkness didn't last long there. Here in Alaska, once the days started to become longer, there was a sense of quickening in the air, a burgeoning sense of growth.

Today was one of my late days at the office. Dr. Johnson kept the clinic open late two days a week to catch all of the patients who couldn't make it during the day. The sun was starting to set, the sky streaked with scarlet and violet, the colors shimmering on the lake. I was told that the Trumpeter swans, the namesake for the lake, would be returning for the spring soon.

Despite my mother's flagging memory, which was skidding sideways more and more every day it seemed, she loved to research things. She always had. She wasn't much of a fan of the Internet, but Emily had bought her a brand new set of bird books with her birthday money. When Emily had done that, I had simply slipped more back into her bank account.

I was so busy juggling too many balls, there was always something to drop. After we had moved here, I should've thought right away that Mom needed a new set of encyclopedias, but I hadn't. Em, bless her big heart, had.

Anyway, Mom had been flipping through her books, looking up all the birds in Alaska, so she'd told me the swans would be returning for the summer soon. She'd also been chatting about some Bird Fest in a town several hours south of us, Diamond Creek. Apparently, she and my father had taken me to the first one the town had ever held the same year we moved away.

I reminded myself to see if we could go there for a day or so. I considered that perhaps we should find a rental with a view of the lake because she'd love that. I idly wondered if Jesse's place had a view of the lake. As the crow flew, the lake was only a few miles from our house, but the trees obscured its view.

The moment Jesse strolled into my thoughts, my mind flashed to last night and then again to that crazy kiss. With a mental shake, I stood from my desk, just as Rachel popped her head around my door.

"Hey," she said with a smile, her ponytail swinging. Closing the door behind her, she stepped inside and leaned her hip on one of the chairs across from my desk. I didn't have many friends here. Like Emily, I was starting from scratch. But Rachel had become a fast one, which was great. Seeing as I spent most of my workdays with her, it was convenient we got along so well. Another bonus was she seemed to know everyone in town because she'd grown up here.

"Were you going to tell me something?" she asked

Leaning my hip against my desk, I picked up a pen, idly flipping it back and forth between my fingers. "Huh?"

She arched a brow, her lips curling in a sly smile. "Sandy mentioned that you asked to have Jesse Franklin switched over to Dr. Johnson. What's that about?"

My cheeks heated, and I cursed my fair skin. Staring at her for a long moment, I finally shrugged. "Well, I don't know if you've heard, but he found my mom yesterday afternoon."

Rachel nodded. "Uh-huh. I know. Holly mentioned that he could barely keep his eyes off of you at the hospital."

Fuck, fuck, fuck. Holly and Rachel were good friends. Downside to small towns was there was no such thing as a secret around here. I chewed on the inside of my cheek, considering whether to tell her about my rather startling and unexpected kiss in the hospital yesterday. Deciding against it quickly, I held her gaze and sort of explained.

"He's my neighbor, and there might be a little something there. Small town or not, it just feels weird to keep him as my patient. Dr. Johnson can handle it, and it's not like it's anything major. It's just his shoulder."

"Oh, I think it's great," Rachel declared firmly.

"What's great?"

"You're totally uptight. You were freaked out just because

he was eyeing your ass the other day. I'm all about you getting that obstacle out of the way. Jesse Franklin is totally hot, and I'm not the only one who thinks he's got the hots for you. Holly does too. I think you should be all over that. He's sex-on-a-stick hot."

Rachel's grin stretched wider. I rolled my eyes, trying to keep a level head. I didn't need to get all excited over a man. Any man. But Jesse was so damned tempting. "You know, my life doesn't exactly leave a lot of room for romance."

"Oh, romance isn't what I'm talking about. You need to get laid."

At that, she spun out of the room, her laugh trailing behind her.

Chapter Seven

JESSE

I stood beside the ambulance, waiting with an elderly woman sitting in the back. Dana Halloran, one of our EMT's and a friend, was checking her lungs and having her breathe into a respirator. Dana gave me a thumbs up, and I nodded, turning away. Our crew had been called to a fire just outside of town. We weren't really into fire season yet, but there was always something.

This elderly woman who lived alone had accidentally set her woodstove pipe on fire. Her small cabin was just isolated enough that we hadn't gotten the call right away, and the home was destroyed. A neighbor had spotted the smoke and flames and called us. Spinning around, I scanned the smoldering remains of the home. The roof was caving in and only two walls were left standing. Ward, our crew superintendent was conferring with Caleb, the other foreman for the crew along with me.

I'd mostly been helping on the sidelines since I had another few days to get cleared for full duty. Striding over to meet them, I checked in. "What's the plan?"

Ward caught my eyes. "Well, the fire's out. Obviously," he

said with a sigh. "I'm going to leave half the crew here with hoses to monitor until it's completely cool. You wanna stay or go?"

Before I could answer, Caleb did. "I'll stay. Jesse stayed late the other night."

Our crew was a solid group. I used to share foreman duties with Susannah, Ward's wife. But she switched over to the local crew from our hotshot crew after she got pregnant. Our crew rotated duties for local calls as well. Caleb had fit in seamlessly. It helped that he'd been born and raised in Willow Brook. He was as solid as they came, a good friend, and he never hesitated to step up.

"Sounds like a plan," I replied. "Looks like Hazel will be fine," I said, referring to the elderly woman who was with Dana.

At Caleb's nod, I turned and started to walk away when Ward called my name. "Yeah?" I asked, glancing back over my shoulder.

"Carrie Dodge called a few minutes ago. Herman's back up in the tree again. If you don't mind swinging by on your way home, that would be great," Ward explained.

With a chuckle, I gave him a thumbs up. "On it."

Carrie was known to all of the firefighters based in Willow Brook. The station served as a base for most of Alaska with two hotshot crews here, along with the local crew. Most of our time during fire season was spent responding to calls wherever we were needed, which often meant weeks in the wilderness. I loved the work, but it was hard and grueling at times.

Carrie often gave us a laugh. Her cat Herman liked to climb trees. A lot. She used to use her late husband's excavator to get Herman out of his jams by herself. Until she and the excavator ended up in a ditch once. The station now "owned" her excavator, but we left it on her property. We left it there for the sole purpose of these calls.

As I drove home, the sun was starting to set in the

distance. Denali stood tall above the landscape, its hulking form dark against the orange and gold sky. It didn't matter that I'd been born and raised in Alaska, I never tired of the views. I'd spent most of my childhood in the Fairbanks area, but my family moved to Willow Brook right after I graduated from high school. When a position opened up on one of the crews here, I jumped on it. Turning my truck onto the road toward Carrie's place, Swan Lake shimmered in the distance, the watercolor sky reflected on its surface. I imagined Herman might enjoy the view from whatever tree he happened to be perched in this evening.

Within minutes, I'd arrived at Carrie's place. She waved from the porch as I climbed in the excavator. Herman was in one of his preferred trees, high in the branches. As soon as the excavator bucket was close enough, he hopped right into it.

In short order, I carried him to Carrie on the porch while he rubbed his chin on my shoulder. "Here's your boy," I said, handing him over.

Carrie smiled and handed me an oatmeal raisin cookie, my favorite. Carrie knew how to bribe us, not that it was necessary.

"Thank you, Jesse."

"Anytime, Carrie. All you have to do is call."

She flashed a grin and immediately started fussing over Herman. With a wave, I left. Once I turned toward the station, my mind spun instantly to Charlie's mother. Unlike the woman we'd helped out of her home today, Olive didn't live alone. She had Charlie and Emily to take care of her.

I couldn't think of Olive without thinking of Charlie. After I'd left the other night, I'd puzzled over my reaction to her. Any desire I had for her should've been snuffed out once I had a clear picture of her life. Far from it. I had no fucking clue what to think about that. I worried she had too much to take care of on her own, and I wanted to help however I could.

It wasn't that I wasn't a helpful guy. Hell, I was a hotshot firefighter. Yet, the idea of helping didn't usually get all tangled up in the crazy, burning need I felt for Charlie. I wasn't much for pondering the idea of a relationship. In fact, I was pretty easy come, easy go when it came to dating.

Yet, the desire I felt with Charlie was unlike anything I'd experienced. This wasn't my first rodeo. I'd had a few semi-serious relationships, but I'd never felt such a strong pull. Instead of the complications of her life driving me away, they drew me in. I admired the hell out of her.

She was smart as hell and obviously cared deeply for her family. Not everyone would step up the way she had for her mother. While I didn't know the story behind how her niece ended up with her, it was just another piece of the puzzle that told me she was an incredibly loyal person. It worried me to see her trying to carry all of those burdens on her own.

With that in mind, I had surreptitiously asked Holly for some advice about ways to get her some help for her mom. As far as I knew, her mom hadn't wandered off again in the last week or so, which was a relief.

Yet, long-term, it was an untenable situation. Much as Emily seemed to be older than her years and more than willing to help out, it didn't make sense for them not to find help. Holly had gotten a gleam in her eyes when I asked. "You like Charlie," she'd said bluntly.

I'd simply shrugged. She was spot on, but I didn't think Charlie would appreciate me gabbing about the fact I happened to think she was sexy as hell.

Holly had filled me in that they'd provided Charlie with a list of possible home care providers, but she was concerned Charlie felt too guilty to follow up on it. I couldn't help but agree. Holly had gone on to say she planned to push the issue and make the referrals herself if Olive wandered off again.

Leaning my palms against the shower wall at the station,

I decided another impromptu visit to Charlie was in order. After I dried off, I zapped off a text to her, letting her know I'd be stopping by with pizza for Emily and her mother. I figured she couldn't say no to that. With Waffle to tagalong with me, I picked up three pizzas because I'd noticed Emily practically ate an entire pizza on her own.

Charlie answered the door, her hair up in a knot. She looked as if she'd just gotten home from the office. She'd chucked her white lab coat, but she had on black slacks and a button down blouse. My eyes were immediately drawn to the valley between her breasts. Because, yeah, I had it that bad.

Damn. If I'd known this was how she looked under her lab coats, I was fairly certain I'd have kissed her the first time I ever laid eyes on her. She was so tempting. Managing to drag my eyes up, I caught her gaze waiting. A flush crested her cheeks. "Hi, I just got your text."

Before I had time for a reply, Emily skidded across the room on her socks, almost bumping into me. I thought she was going to take the pizza, but her entire focus was on Waffle. With barely a greeting to me, she dashed off to fling herself on the floor on a small circular rug in front of the couch where Waffle obligingly followed.

Catching Charlie's eyes, I smiled. "How's it going?"

Opening the door wide, she gestured me through. "Oh, you know. Busy day at work. Every day when Mom doesn't wander off, I figure that's a win."

Following her across the living room into the kitchen, I glanced around, wondering where her mother was and fighting the urge to slide my hand down her spine. She looked weary, and I wanted to pull her close and tell her it would all be okay. I distantly wondered if I'd lost my ever-loving mind.

Thank fuck I had something to do with my hands. Setting the pizzas down, I looked over where she stood by the refrigerator. "Beer? Wine?"

"Beer will do. Every time," I said simply.

When she flashed a small smile my way, my cock twitched. I sternly ordered it to behave. Charlie handed me a beer after removing the cap. She poured herself a glass of wine before turning around and leaning her hips against the counter, her eyes scanning the living room area.

"Em would love it if you'd just leave Waffle here," she said with a little chuckle.

I looked over to see Emily stretched out on the rug, petting Waffle. Waffle, of course, would probably be happy to stay here. She was attached enough to me, but she was a total attention whore.

Catching Charlie's eyes, I shrugged. "She can come visit whenever you want. Where's your mom?"

"She's asleep. She sleeps a lot," she said softly. "I was going to text you and tell you not to bring too much pizza but..." Her words trailed off as her gaze flicked to the three boxes.

"No worries. I'm sure Emily will eat the leftovers, right?"

Charlie laughed softly, the sound low and melodic. Fuck me. Even her laugh was sexy. I couldn't quite believe that I'd been nothing more than annoyed with her when I first met her. But I could chalk that up to being annoyed about my shoulder. I suddenly remembered something.

"Hey, when Sandy called to remind me about our appointment, she said I was scheduled with Dr. Johnson."

Charlie's cheeks flushed. Okay, this was officially ridiculous. All she had to do was blush and blood shot to my groin. If she hadn't blushed, I might've bought her excuse.

"Oh, it's nothing. Just an availability thing."

I held her gaze, taking a slow swallow of my beer. "You're lying." I couldn't keep the grin from tugging at the corners of my mouth.

Her cheeks were stained pink, the flush deepening as she looked at me. She took a gulp of her wine and gave her head a little shake. I'd have given anything to climb inside her mind and see just what she was thinking right then.

"Fine. I think it's best if you see Dr. Johnson."

"Why?"

Her lips tightened and her eyes narrowed as she looked at me. I was pushing her, and I damned well knew it. But I didn't care. I was going to make her explain.

"Jesse, you know," she murmured quickly before she took another sip of wine.

"No, actually I don't. I wouldn't be asking if I did." I didn't quite know why I needed her to be straight with me on this, but I did. I supposed it might have had something to do with the fact I could hardly stop thinking about her, and I wanted to know if she maybe, just maybe, had the same issue with me.

She glanced over to Emily and Waffle and then back to me before angling her body toward me. "Jesse, do I have to spell it out? You kissed me. I can't have a professional relationship with you and kiss you," she hissed.

"Oh, it wasn't a one-way street, you kissed me too," I countered.

She almost spit out the wine she'd just sipped. She snagged a paper towel off the roll mounted above the counter. After quickly wiping her lips, she dabbed at the drop of wine that landed on her neck and was rolling down between her breasts.

I'd have given just about anything to lick that. While I might have been having naughty thoughts, I wasn't going to do anything about it in front of our audience.

"Fine. So I did," she said quickly as if that was the end of the conversation

Oh, hell no. Holding her gaze for a long moment, I shook my head slowly. "Why should it matter? If it was just one kiss, there's no reason to worry. I promise to be nothing but professional. Unless you were hoping for more..."

Her nostrils flared as she took a deep breath, which also

conveniently stretched her blouse across her breasts. Her nipples were taut, pressing against the thin fabric.

After a moment, she laughed. "I can't do this conversation. Not right now."

That was enough for me.

———

I carried the last plate over to the dishwasher, pausing for a moment to enjoy the sight of Charlie bent over the dishwasher as she put the silverware in the basket. I had some ideas, and I wasn't about to walk away tonight without more of a taste of her.

The house was quiet. Charlie had checked on her mother a bit ago and reported her sound asleep, while Emily had gone off to bed as well. Charlie straightened, and I handed the plate to her. After putting it in the rack, she closed the dishwasher, tapping the button to start it. A soft hum filled the room.

She turned to face me, curling her hands on the edge of the counter. Her lips parted and her breath came out softly. Somewhere along the way tonight while I'd been busy being nothing but appropriate in front of Emily, Charlie had pulled the pins out of her hair. It fell around her shoulders now. She'd also changed out of her slacks into a pair of cotton pants. They rested low on her hips and swung around her ankles. Yet, she'd kept her blouse on, which only tempted me to unbutton it.

I took a step, closing the distance between us. I expected her to maybe, just maybe, shimmy away from me. But she didn't.

She simply looked at me. Her sharp features were softened with her hair down, and her cheeks pinkened as we stared at each other.

"So, I'll see Dr. Johnson from now on. Does that mean I get more than one kiss?"

With every word I spoke, the flush deepened on her cheeks. I could see the rapid flutter of her pulse along the downy skin of her neck. With any other woman, I would've thought this was just a little fun. But with Charlie, I felt electrified. My need for her was so intense, I'd have to beat it back with a stick to stop it.

She caught the corner of her bottom lip with her teeth, worrying it. I thought she was thinking, but that only served to ratchet up the need lashing at me. She caught my eyes and I saw something flicker in the depths. It disappeared as quickly as it came, but it made my heart squeeze. That unfamiliar need to protect, to try to ease the burdens she carried, rose inside in response to whatever I'd seen in her eyes.

"My life is kind of messy," she finally said softly.

"Isn't everyone's?" I countered.

A startled laugh escaped. "I'm pretty sure not everyone moved all the way across the country to try to make their mom happy, only to find out she was already too senile to enjoy it. I'm also pretty sure not everyone is taking a crash course in parenting a 15-year-old who's pretty cranky most of the time. That's what I mean by messy," she said bluntly.

"I know all that, tell me something new." I distantly wondered why I wasn't reacting to these details. They were the plain circumstances of her life, yet they didn't rattle me. Rather, they fed into my drive to protect her, which in turn, fed into my need for her.

She still didn't move and her breath came in shallow puffs. It was taking all I had not to kiss her. But I didn't.

"That's not enough?" she asked.

"To chase me away?"

Another startled laugh slipped out. She snatched up her almost empty wine glass on the counter beside her, gulping it down quickly. The last drop escaped, and she caught it with the tip of her tongue, which only tightened the need coiling inside of me.

"Well, I think any sane man would run," she finally said.

"Well, then I guess I'm crazy."

I closed the distance between us and fit my mouth over hers. The moment my lips met hers, she stiffened for a flash, the air nearly electric around us, and then she let out a low moan, opening her mouth and inviting me in. Her hand slid up to cup my nape, gripping my hair tightly. I swept my tongue into the warm welcome of her mouth, a sweet, wild heat. We kissed hungrily, greedy for each other. What I meant to be just a kiss, just like the need beating like a drum in my body, it became so much more than that.

Because, you see, with Charlie, there was no calculation. Whatever it was between us, the force was beyond my control. Threading a hand into her hair, I nearly devoured her mouth. I dimly realized I was gripping the edge of the counter tightly. Releasing my hand, I slid it down her spine, so I could cup her sweet ass and rock my arousal into her.

We were practically feral. Her leg curled around my calf, and she flexed into me. Her hand slid up under my shirt, the feel of her palm against me sending little lightning bolts everywhere under the surface of my skin.

Waffle gave a soft woof, the sound barely breaking through the fog of need. My mind was hazed with nothing more than an intense yearning for Charlie. Tearing free of our kiss, I let my forehead fall against hers, murmuring, "I think Waffle hears something."

Opening my eyes, I found her smoky gaze waiting. A soft sound came from her throat, my heart kicking against my ribs in reply. She laughed, a raspy low chuckle.

Gathering myself, I lifted my head and glanced over my shoulder. It must've been a dream because Waffle was sound asleep again, one of her back legs kicking in her sleep.

"I probably..." Charlie's words trailed off.

I sensed she was about to tell me this probably shouldn't happen in the kitchen with her mother and niece upstairs.

"Walk with me," I said. "It's okay for you to leave for a little bit, right?"

She held my gaze, her eyes assessing. I didn't know what she saw there. All I knew was I wanted her. After a moment, she nodded. "For a little bit. Em's fifteen, she'd rather have the house to herself every night, and Mom's out once she's in bed. But not long," she cautioned.

I lifted a hand, brushing her hair out of her eyes, catching sight of that streak of purple. "I didn't mean for you to spend the night. My place is only a five-minute walk away. You can walk Waffle home with me."

We were talking, but leaving some things blank. The blanks were already filled in my mind.

"Okay," she said slowly. "I can walk Waffle home with you."

As I sifted my fingers through her hair, I caught the purple streak and twined it around my finger. "Where did this come from?"

"Emily did it. I was trying to bond with her. I like it," she said with a soft smile.

"I love it," I replied. I didn't say aloud that it reminded me of kissing her. On the outside, she was uptight, but when she let down her guard, she was like sweet fire.

Chapter Eight

CHARLIE

We walked through the falling darkness with Waffle bounding ahead. The air was crisp and chilly, winter holding onto it by the teeth until spring could snatch it back.

Stars spread across the sky, glittering like diamonds. Our breath was misty in the air. I was so hot inside, I barely noticed the chill. I idly wondered if I was half out of my mind.

A small part of my brain was squeaking that I needed to hurry back home. The more rational part reminded me that I went to work every day, and Emily went to school. I could be gone for a little while. Considering that I'd set up an alarm on the home, which would alert my phone when any doors were opened, I knew it was fine to leave. Em had been all on board with that plan. If I'd worried she was the kind of kid to try to sneak out on her own, I now knew that was a pointless worry.

I supposed I was freaking out because the need spinning through my veins almost frightened me with its intensity. It was born from a part of myself I had shut down so fiercely under the weight after my father and sister had died.

Layering on top of that was learning how to hold together what little was left of my family. What a hodgepodge we were.

I had missed, desperately missed, being carefree. With Jesse's hand warm around mine, his grip strong and firm, I simply walked with him. We hadn't spoken further. I wanted to tumble into this fire between us and forget, even if only for a little while, the weariness I'd been carrying inside for so long.

Not that I had doubted him, but I was surprised when we came into a clearing within a few minutes. There was a path from our house to his through the trees. I guessed it had been there for a long time with other neighbors meandering between homes.

As though he read my mind, he spoke, "That's an old ski trail. It carries on past to the other side of your property as well. This area used to be owned by a single family." He paused, gesturing in the direction where the road ended. "They used to have trails all over and let people ski here. That was before I even moved here, but I learned about it when I bought my property."

Nodding, I looked up at the sky and inhaled a breath of crisp air. A half moon hung over the mountains in the distance, casting enough silvery light in the sky for the hulking shape of the mountains to be illuminated in the darkness.

Waffle had run ahead and was waiting on a back deck. There was just enough light with my eyes adjusted to the darkness to see his home. It was a medium-sized, single-story house. The roof came up to a low point in the center of the roofline. Still holding my hand, Jesse walked me through the backyard onto the deck. Floor to ceiling windows ran along the length of the deck with a pair of French doors in the middle.

He opened a door, and Waffle dashed through. As we stepped inside, two lamps came on in the back corner and a light overhead, offering a soft glow in the room. I presumed the lights were set on motion detectors. Glancing around, I took in the space. We'd entered into the living room. There was a sectional couch with a television mounted on the wall to one side and a small woodstove in the back corner.

To the other side where the hardwood floor met tile was the kitchen. A counter ran along the back wall with the sink in the center, the dishwasher to one side and the refrigerator to the other. Opposite that was a curved island, which served as a divider between the rooms. On one side was the stovetop and oven, and on the other, stools for seating.

The colors were basic, everything a soft gray. Catching his eyes, I smiled. "This is nice," I said, my voice sounding loud in the quiet room.

He shrugged. "Thanks. I had it built by a local crew—Amelia and Lucy. They run Kick Ass Construction and happen to be friends of mine."

I'd seen the sign for the company downtown, but I hadn't known it was run by women. I laughed, liking the idea. "Well, they do nice work," I said, scanning the rest of the space. To the back were a doorway and a small hallway where I could see several doors on either side.

When my eyes landed on Jesse's again, his gaze darkened. "So..." he said softly.

I didn't know what to say, but nothing more than the sound of his voice sent my belly into a flip.

Waffle trotted over to a water bowl by the kitchen counter. After lapping it quickly, she meandered down the hall, her tail swaying. She disappeared through a doorway. Jesse caught my eyes, his mouth curling at the corner and promptly sending flutters spinning in my belly.

"She likes the bed in the guest room," he said with a chuckle. "It's pretty much her own bed."

"Oh," was my brilliant response.

Sensation was prickling over my skin at his nearness. Mingling with that was a rushing sense of uncertainty. My mind was so accustomed to constantly worrying—about work, about my mom, about Em. Letting my worries go, even if only for a little while, seemed foreign. The hamster in my brain was used to running overtime on the spinning wheel of my thoughts. I wondered if I even knew how to even do this anymore. *This* being anything remotely related to desire.

I hoped it was a bit like riding a bike.

I didn't realize I'd spoken aloud until Jesse's grin stretched from one side of his mouth to the other. "I think it probably is," he murmured.

His gaze searched my face, his grin slowly fading.

"I can walk you back home," he said, his tone low and quiet.

Holding his gaze, I tried to take a slow breath. But with my heart pounding hard and fast, I couldn't quite get that much air inside my lungs. I realized he was picking up on my anxiety. Because he was decent guy, he was giving me an out, a perfectly easy out.

As deep as my anxiety ran, it couldn't override the need rushing through me like a river in spring. I'd watched the water pouring down over a cliff on a mountainside the other day and been amazed at its force and speed. I felt like that inside. As if my body had been frozen and quiet, and now it was thawing and everything was running wild.

Even if it was only once, even if it was awkward later, I could give myself this. Because nothing had chipped through the ice of my defenses the way Jesse had. Looking back at him, I shook my head. "No, you can walk me home later." And then I caught his hand in mine and tugged him toward me.

Just like that, I forgot everything else.

Our mouths collided, and it was like getting caught in the center of the flame. We practically devoured each other. For me, there was an intense, driving need, specifically for him. My need was crashing up against the reality that I hadn't had anything other than a solo sexual experience in over three years. I climbed him like a tree, my hand sliding up around his nape, gripping his shaggy curls. I curled my foot around his calf as my hands got busy mapping his chest. He was one hell of a man— all hard muscle, every inch of him.

Jesse was just as greedy as me, his tongue sweeping into my mouth with a low growl as he held me in place and kissed me as if his life depended on it. In this moment, everything depended on falling into this fire. It was a rough, almost painful kiss. I felt the sting on my scalp when his hand tangled in my hair. When he broke free, he dusted damp kisses along my neck, sending hot shivers through me.

My panties were wet, and I rocked my hips to relieve the ache building at my core. Feeling his arousal hot at the apex of my thighs, I almost cried out when his hand slid down my back to cup my bottom and lift me up against him.

He held me easily, but then that wasn't surprising. The man was nothing but raw masculinity. He murmured something against my skin, the feel of his lips alone sending jolts of fire through me.

"What?" I gasped.

He lifted his head as he turned and carried me over towards the couch. "I said my shoulder's fine. Can't you tell?"

The devilish glint in his eyes and the curl of his lips sent my belly into a free fall, fierce desire rushing through me, hot and intense.

I laughed softly. "I suppose it is. It has been almost two weeks."

"If Doc doesn't clear me when I see him, I'm going to make him talk to you," he teased.

I managed to tease right back. "I suppose it's good I had enough sense to move you back to his schedule."

Jesse's eyes darkened. He leaned forward as he reached the couch, easing my hips onto the back of it. My knees fell open, and he stepped right between them. His eyes flicked down, and I literally felt the burn of his gaze on my breasts. My nipples tightened, perking up just for him. His fingers loosened in my hair, trailing along the side of my neck and down in between my breasts. He made quick work of my blouse.

"I've been wanting to unbutton this all night," he murmured, the roughened edges of his voice a lash against the need building inside of me.

I gasped when my blouse fell open, the cool air hitting my skin and tightening my nipples to an ache. He traced over the silk of my bra, his touch light but like fire on my skin. I cried out when he squeezed my nipple.

"Charlie..." he murmured.

Dragging my eyes up, I found his dark green gaze waiting, the need contained there reflecting back to me. As out of control as I felt, it was a relief to see that he might be somewhere on that edge with me.

Tracing a finger around a nipple, he watched as I arched into him and then his lips were on mine again. With a flick of his thumb between my breasts, my bra fell open and my breasts tumbled free from the silk, hot, tight, and achy.

I needed more. I needed to feel him against me.

The next few moments were a rush as I tugged at his shirt, and he reached behind his neck to lift it off in one swoop. Inside of a few seconds, his shirt fell into a rumple on the floor with my blouse. He lifted me from the couch—holding me with one arm, he was that strong—and yanked my sweat pants down. As I kicked them free, he eased me back onto the couch. Once again, he was standing between my knees, his hot skin against my breasts.

The feeling of all that muscle pressed against me had me out of my mind. I was gasping and arching into him, near frantic from the lust streaking through me.

I didn't know if it was because it had been just too damn long since I'd been with anyone, or if the attraction between us burned that intensely. All I knew was I needed him so fiercely, I was burning up. There was nothing graceful about it. I yanked at the buttons on his fly as he dragged his fingers over the silk between my thighs. I was slick with need, my panties drenched with it.

I cried out when he pushed the silk to the side, his fingers trailing through my folds before he sank two inside of me. I was tight, and I didn't even care. I needed more. Dragging my palm over his briefs, I shoved his jeans out of the way. When I slipped my hand into his briefs as I pushed them down around his hips and curled my palm around his cock, he muttered something against my skin as his teeth closed over my nipple. Hot, dirty words.

"Charlie, you're so fucking sexy..."

His words trailed off into a low groan. I wasn't used to hearing myself described that way. I loved it. As he stroked his fingers in and out of me, pleasure spun tighter and tighter inside. Everything he said was like pouring gas on the fire, the flames licking inside of me.

"So wet, can't wait to feel this around my cock..."

I was riding his hand, my hips bucking into him. His thumb swirled over my clit, pressing down, and I fractured inside, nearly shouting his name as my channel clenched around his fingers. My climax rushed through me, pleasure sending sparks scattering inside. I was nearly limp by the time it was over, curling boneless against him.

Then, he was lifting me into his arms, turning to walk around the sectional and sit down with me a bundle in his lap. He produced a condom after yanking his wallet out of his pocket, shoving his briefs out of the way and rolling it on in record time.

My brain was a haze of pleasure and passion. With need still pounding through my body, I dragged my eyes open. Just looking at him kindled the fire inside all over again. He was so ridiculously handsome with his tousled curls, his dark green eyes, and the strong features of his face.

My eyes flicked down, absorbing the sight of his glorious

muscled chest. For these few stolen moments out of time, it was mine to explore. I trailed my hand along his jaw line and down over his chest. His breath hissed through his teeth when I trailed my fingers down over his abs and lightly gripped his cock.

"I need to be inside of you," he murmured, his voice tight.

I rose up, straddling him. He positioned his cock at my entrance, nudging in slightly. I sank down slowly, taking him inside my tight clench, crying out as he filled me. The fit was snug, but it was *so* good. The delicious stretch of him filling me brought me right back to the edge.

Chapter Nine

JESSE

Charlie sank down over me, taking me inside of her core, inch by inch. Every inch tight, hot, and slick. She was drenched, so slippery wet, I slid in easily. "So fucking good," I murmured.

Glancing up at her, I soaked her in. She was glorious. Her hair was a wild tousle around her shoulders, her breasts playing peekaboo with long, dark locks falling over them. I couldn't have said what I'd expected with her, but it wasn't this wild, thrumming, out of control madness.

Her hips settled onto me when I was buried to the hilt inside of her. I wanted to see her fly apart again because watching her last orgasm was the hottest thing I'd ever seen. I forced myself to hold still because the frayed thread of control I was clinging to was about to snap.

After a beat, I slid my hands down her sides and gripped her hips. She started to move slowly, and I rocked with her. Inside of a hot second, pleasure was lashing at me, whipping me hotter and hotter, faster and faster. She rode me, rolling up and sinking down, her channel pulsing around me.

Her breasts rubbed against my chest as I tried to hang

onto my control. My head fell back on a groan. I was almost there, but I wasn't letting go until she found her own release again. Reaching between us, I pressed my thumb over her clit. She cried out, her body going taut and her channel clamping down hard over my cock and pulling me over the edge with her.

My release came so hard and fast, I lost my breath and distantly heard myself calling her name. She fell against me, tucking her head into the dip on my neck. It felt as if we'd run a race. I could barely catch my breath and listened as hers gusted against my skin.

After several moments, I felt Charlie lift her head. Her hair slipped through my fingers when her eyes caught mine. I wasn't quite sure how to read her expression.

"Well," she said softly.

"Well is right," I replied.

We simply looked at each other for a long moment before she straightened. I found I didn't want to move. At all.

I was unprepared for any of this. I sure as hell hadn't expected to have this little interlude tonight. I wouldn't deny I'd wanted it. Badly. Yet, now we faced the potentially awkward part. Not for me, but I sensed it might be for Charlie.

"I'll walk you home," I said.

Those gray eyes with just a hint of violet in them widened as she looked at me. "You don't need to do that. It's just a few minutes away."

"It's probably smart. I'm not worried you'll get lost, but there are moose and bears around. If there's two of us, it's less likely they'll be bothered."

Her eyes widened further and then she smiled. My heart gave a resounding thump. I loved it when she smiled. She sat there on my lap with me still buried inside of her, with her nipples pink and still puckered tight, and her hair a wild tangle. She was everything I wanted and more.

"But then you'll be walking home alone," she countered.

"We'll take Waffle with us."

She chuckled, and I wished she laughed more. She slowly rose up. We untangled ourselves and put our clothes back on.

In short order, we were stepping onto the back deck with Waffle roused from her slumber. She'd looked puzzled at first, but the moment I headed toward the door she leapt up, awake instantly. We walked through the starry night, our breath misting the early spring air. I left Charlie at her door, unable to resist one more kiss.

Returning home, I fell asleep with the taste of her on my lips.

———

A few days later, I went in for my appointment with Dr. Johnson. I happened to see Charlie stepping into one of the examination rooms with another patient. Her eyes caught mine briefly, her cheeks pinkening before she turned away.

Much as I would've rather seen her for my pesky shoulder, I realized it made sense for her to keep that line clear. She was nothing if not professional. In the days since our mutual collision of bodies, I'd felt a tug over toward her place every day. The only thing holding me back was the reality that she wasn't living alone. Not to say that I had a problem with her niece or her mother, but it wasn't like I could just show up and bend her over the counter like I wanted.

The moment Dr. Johnson entered the room where I was waiting, he lifted a bushy gray brow and eyed me. "Don't know how you ended up back with me boy," he said gruffly.

I shrugged, hewing to vague. "I suppose Dr. Lane was busy."

"Of course, she's busy," he muttered. "Let me take a look at that shoulder."

He rolled my shoulder a few times and had me do a few strength tests. There wasn't even a twinge of pain. It actually felt a bit stronger as well. All in all, I took that as a good sign. He asked me a few chatty questions, and I took my opening to see what he might tell me about Charlie. "How long has Dr. Lane been here anyway?"

"About six months, give or take. I hope to retire next year, so I'm hoping she stays on. Still looking for someone else to help out."

There was a knock on the door and a nurse poked her head in to tell Doc his next patient was there. He waved me off, assuring me I was cleared for full duty and then left. As I walked down the hall, my eyes caught on the door that I knew led to Charlie's office. Glancing around, I saw no one happened to be in the hallway. With a quick knock, I opened it, hoping to find her in there. I was in luck. She stood by her desk, her hand curled over the edge as she spoke on the phone.

"Em, I'm just saying that before I say it's okay to spend the night, I want to talk to her mother."

I couldn't hear the other side of the conversation, but I could imagine the argument. It was then that Charlie turned around, her eyes widening and a flush cresting on her cheeks. "Em, I have to go. I'll call you back in a little bit."

She hung up quickly, tossing her phone on the desk. "Oh my God, you'd think I just ended her world," she said with a sigh as she pushed her glasses up on her nose.

I'd forgotten how much I loved her in glasses. With a shake, I forced myself to focus.

"What happened?"

Charlie leaned her hips on her desk, turning to face me more fully. "She wants to spend the weekend at a friend's house, but I haven't had a chance to talk to the parents, so... Well, you can guess how she took that. I'll have to scout up their contact info and call them. I would love for her to spend the weekend with a friend. I just need to do my due diligence. She says that's boring and nosy."

"What's her friend's name?"

"Kayla Becker."

"Oh, I know her parents. They're good people. Hang on, I might even have their number in my phone."

"How...?" Her question trailed off as I flicked my eyes back up to hers.

"I've lived here longer than you, and I'm a firefighter. We know everybody."

She laughed. "Is that so?"

"Hazard of the job. They actually live near my parents."

Scrolling through my contacts, I recited the number when I found it. "Let me call over right now and introduce you." I didn't wait for Charlie's reply and quickly dialed. Janice, Kayla's mother, answered. "Hey, Janice, it's Jesse. Kind of an odd request, but Charlie Lane is Emily..." I paused and glanced to Charlie, wondering if Emily shared her last name. Charlie mouthed "Lane." "Emily Lane's aunt. Anyway, apparently Kayla invited her to spend the weekend there. I told Charlie I knew your number, so I called."

Janice laughed. "Oh, perfect. I was just asking Kayla how to reach Emily's mom. But you say it's her aunt?"

This was where I had a rather large blank in my knowledge of Charlie and how she came to be taking care of her niece. I knew her sister and her father died, but that was it. I certainly didn't think it was my place to share that right now. "How about you just talk to her? I figured I could connect you two."

Charlie took the phone from me and quickly spoke with Janice. Inside of a few minutes, they had chatted and Charlie was telling Janice what time she'd drop off Emily. After she hung up and handed the phone over, she sighed. "Thank you. Now I can give Em some good news. Let me call her real quick if you don't mind."

"Of course not." Seeing as I'd barged into her office, I

was just glad she hadn't kicked me out yet. I strode to the windows, looking out at the mountains in the distance. Charlie called Emily, her tone of voice alone cuing me that Emily was pleased with the turn of events.

After she ended the call, Charlie came to stand beside me at the window, turning and leaning her hips against the windowsill. I'd wondered over the last few days how my body would react when I saw her again. I'd had this idea that perhaps I'd slaked my pounding need for her. Definitely not. Even now, in her white lab coat that effectively shielded her delectable body from my eyes, she was so fucking hot.

Her hair was pulled back tightly again, that streak of purple almost hidden amongst the dark locks. She adjusted her glasses again, and blood shot to my groin.

Damn. This wasn't anything I'd expected. But then nothing about Charlie Lane was anything I had *ever* expected.

"I don't suppose you know anything about Bird Fest," she said.

The shift in topic only briefly threw me. Rallying and yanking my mind out of the gutter, I nodded. "I do. It's an annual bird watching festival down in Diamond Creek. That's about four hours south of here, give or take. Why do you ask?"

"My mom loves birds, and she wants to go. I guess it's this weekend," she said with a rueful grin.

"I'll take you. We can make it a day trip."

Charlie stared at me for a beat, her eyes widening, and a little laugh escaping. "Are you serious?"

I didn't know why, but it rubbed me the wrong way for her to be so startled that I would offer that. Maybe we had gotten off on the wrong start because I'd met her when I had an injured shoulder. I'd seen her as the obstacle to me getting back to work. But I was a decent guy. I'd be happy to take them. It was a beautiful drive.

"Of course I am," I replied, ignoring the questioning voice in the back of my mind.

I'd just proposed something that could be seen as a date. I had hardly stopped thinking about Charlie since the other night. The only factor keeping this from being an actual date was the fact her mother would be coming along with us. Yet, somehow that also made it feel more intimate.

None of this was in my typical wheelhouse.

Charlie's eyes narrowed, her gaze sobering. "Look, it's really nice of you to ask, but this is my mom we're talking about. It seems…"

I shook my head sharply, her words trailing off when I did. "It's a gorgeous drive. We can grab lunch down there and spend the day. It's not a hardship. Believe me. If your mom wants to go, she should see it." I didn't say aloud the obvious. There might not be many more years her mother would be able to go.

Charlie was quiet and then a small smile graced her face. "Okay. My mom will love it, and I don't know where the hell I'm going."

Chapter Ten

CHARLIE

"Em, time to go," I called up the stairs.

I put the last dish in the dishwasher and closed it before hurrying up the stairs to check on my mom. Poking my head around the corner of her bedroom door, I found her sound asleep.

I was considering whether I should wake her up to take her with us. Although the drive over to Emily's friend's place wasn't too far, I worried when my mother was home alone. Even though I'd set up the alert system for the doors, I still worried. Thank goodness she remained functional as far as her daily living activities. She had no trouble with showering, dressing herself, and taking care of her meals. The main worry was her wandering out of the house.

She was sound asleep though and sleeping more and more these days. My heart gave a squeeze of sadness, and I quietly closed the door. It wasn't as if I didn't know she would sleep more, given her age and current mental state, yet every sign reminded me of where she was headed and what it meant. It made my heart ache. I jotted her a note and left it on the counter in case she came downstairs while I was gone with Emily.

Returning upstairs, I could hear Emily rustling around in her bedroom and gave a quick knock on the door.

"Come in," she called.

Opening the door, I found her standing beside her bed, pawing through her backpack.

"Ready?" I asked.

She glanced up. "I can't find my headphones."

"You need your headphones?"

Em sighed and then nodded frantically. "Of course I do."

I wasn't exactly a technological dinosaur, but I still puzzled over how teens these days would hang out together with their faces glued to their phones and hardly acknowledging each other.

"Where were they last?"

We quickly walked her through her afternoon, and she found them in the bathroom. I got a hug for helping her. Those were a refreshing breath of air to her sullen silences, so I squeezed hard before stepping back.

"Okay, let's go."

On the way over to her friend's place, Emily was quiet, her gaze trained out the window. I was beyond happy she had made a friend. I wanted to comment on it, but I knew she didn't appreciate comments on social matters.

"So what are you gonna do this weekend?" she asked out of the blue.

Her question startled me. "Actually, I'm going to take grandma down to a bird watching festival, that one she's been talking about. Jesse offered to take us."

I was rolling to a stop at a stop sign and felt Emily's gaze on me. Glancing over, I found her wide eyes staring at me. "What?"

"Wow," was all she said.

"What do you mean?"

"Well, that's kind of a *thing*."

"A thing?"

She nodded vigorously. "Uh huh. He likes you. I can't believe he's taking you and grandma. That's, like, really nice."

I felt my cheeks heat. Because whether or not Jesse liked me, all I could think about was the other night with him. I managed to keep my expression calm, or so I thought. I simply shrugged. Her eyes widened, a grin tugging at the corners of her mouth.

I kept on driving. Following Janice's directions, I turned down the driveway to their home.

"Are you guys, like, dating?" Em asked.

Taking a deep breath, I shook my head. "He's taking us to see the Bird Fest. That'll be fun for grandma and that's what matters."

The driveway wound ahead of us through the trees. Em was quiet for a beat and then spoke again, "How much longer do you think she'll be able to do stuff like that?"

The driveway ended in a circle in front of the home. Rolling to a stop, I glanced over to her. "I don't know," I said softly, emotion tightening in my throat. This was different than the grief of watching my father die and my sister waste away from cancer. It felt as if we were saying goodbye to my mother one piece at a time.

Em's eyes glistened with tears. I reached across the console and hugged her. She didn't resist and squeezed me tightly. Leaning away, she sniffled and opened the glove box.

"Why is it called a glove box?" she asked suddenly.

Looking over, I laughed. She needed something to shift the topic, and this did it.

"Because when they invented cars, people wore gloves for driving, and they kept them in the glove box."

Em seemed to like that, smiling widely as she blew her nose and dragged her sleeve across her eyes. "Okay. Thanks for letting me spend the night here."

"It's the whole weekend. Remember?"

Her smile expanded. "I know."

Leaning over, she kissed my cheek and then hopped out of the car. Watching her walk in, my heart gave a squeeze. I hadn't quite been prepared to be a parent when Em became mine, yet while I might've been fumbling my way through it, I hoped she would be okay.

———

Later that evening, I was putzing around the kitchen when there was a knock on the door. Striding over, I opened it to find Jesse on the other side. The moment I saw him, butterflies spun in my belly. Because I was that ridiculous.

"Hi," I said, surprised I even managed that.

He grinned, promptly sending my pulse off to the races again and heat blooming in my core.

"Thought I'd check in and see what time you wanted to leave tomorrow," he said easily.

I decided not to point out he could've simply called or texted. Stepping back, I gestured him inside. "Where's Waffle?"

"Sound asleep," he said with a chuckle. "Some days she spends the day with a friend of mine who got one of her puppies. She's tired after that."

"Puppies?"

"Oh yeah. When I got her, she turned out to be pregnant. Her puppies are all around town, and a few ended up with friends."

"Oh."

I was back to my brilliant conversational skills.

"Where's your mom?"

"Asleep. She sleeps a lot."

Wow. Two sentences, including one with more than a single word.

We were still standing by the door. He slipped one hand in his pocket, running the other through his hair. "I suppose that's good, right?"

I shrugged. "I don't have to worry then. Em is off at her friend's and tickled to pieces about it."

Turning away, if only because I needed to do something, I walked toward the kitchen. "Would you like something to drink?"

"Sure," he replied. "Beer if you have it."

"Of course I have it.

I fetched a beer for him and poured myself a glass of wine. He slipped onto one of the stools by the counter, so I joined him, taking a sip of my wine and wondering just what was in store for us tomorrow.

"So what time should we leave?" I asked.

"Well, I checked the schedule. I'm thinking early if you can handle it, let's leave at six," he replied, a gleam in his eyes.

I took a sip of my wine, a grin tugging at the corners of my mouth. "Of course I can handle it. I did eighteen-hour shifts during my residency and slept at the hospital for crying out loud. I can handle getting up at 6 AM. I'm usually up early anyway."

"And your mom?' he asked before taking a swallow of his beer.

My eyes flicked to his fingers, remembering the feel of them buried inside of me. Just that thought and slick need coiled inside. I forgot he had asked a question until he arched a brow and cocked his head to the side.

"Oh, she'll be fine. Even if she's not awake when we're ready to go, she gets up easy. She'll be showered and dressed and ready within about fifteen minutes from when I wake her up."

"Sounds like a plan then. I figure we'll get there around ten. We can spend the morning doing the bird thing, maybe have lunch somewhere near the harbor, and then leave by four. That'll get us back here before it's too late."

"There's a harbor there?"

Jesse cracked a grin. "Of course there is—Otter Cove

Harbor. Diamond Creek is on Kachemak Bay, so plenty of boats are in and out of the harbor all day. I'm guessing most of the bird watching happens near the harbor beaches. It's gorgeous there."

"My mom will be beside herself." I paused and took a sip of my wine. "Thank you."

"For what?"

"Offering to take us down there. It'll make her day. Actually, it'll probably make her year. It's not like I couldn't take her myself, but it's nice to have company. Plus you know where you're going and I don't."

His eyes held mine for a beat. I wasn't quite sure how to interpret what was flickering in their depths. He opened his mouth and then closed it, giving his head a shake. "You're welcome," he finally said.

"Another thing," I said.

He leaned his head back, taking a long swallow of his beer. Leveling his gaze with mine, he asked, "What's that?"

"I kind of thought you were a jerk at first, but I was wrong."

I'd been meaning to say something and not just because I totally had the hots for him. I had read him wrong, completely wrong.

For a beat, he looked surprised at my comment, and then a slow grin stretched across his face. "Ah, I had to work for that."

His words and the look in his eyes sent a flush straight through me.

"Hey, that's not what I meant."

He chuckled, sending my belly spinning in into flips. "I know, but you gave me an opening."

My cheeks got hot. Because that was what Jesse did to me. My body was just all aflutter whenever he was near. Hot and bothered didn't quite capture it.

"I did," I finally said unable to keep from giggling.

"Yeah, and then you dumped me as a patient," he added.

I rolled my eyes. "Hey, I already explained that. How is your shoulder anyway?"

"It's perfectly fine. Dr. Johnson cleared me for full duty, in case you were wondering."

"I was actually. I realized today you were probably there for your appointment, but I got distracted."

"By me?" he asked hopefully.

I burst out laughing. "Maybe, but you were there, so you also know Em had me distracted before I even saw you. Speaking of that, thanks again for connecting me with Kayla's mom. It's been hard for Em to make friends since we moved here. She's on the shy side."

Jesse nodded. "No problem, it won't be too long before you know just as many people as I do. Willow Brook's too small to hide."

"How long have you lived here?"

"My parents moved here right after I graduated from high school in Fairbanks. I was headed into college and then off to my hotshot training. I only made it here about seven years ago."

"Fairbanks?"

"Yep, that's where I grew up. If you can believe it, my parents were tired of the long winters," he said with a chuckle.

"Well, Fairbanks is a good eight hours north of here. It stands to reason it would be warmer here. That's the equivalent of going from Boston to, say, Virginia. Virginia's winters are definitely milder," I offered.

Jesse watched me, a smile playing at his lips. I wanted to know what he was thinking.

He answered for me when he set his beer down and stood to step between my knees and pulled me close. I bumped into him softly, my nipples tightening the moment they met the hard planes of his chest. No matter what I told myself I should or shouldn't do, when it came to Jesse, my body had its own ideas.

"What?" I asked.

"I love how smart you are," he murmured, lifting a hand and sliding his fingers through my hair.

"I was just making an observation about the distance," I murmured.

"Oh, I know. It just made me think. You're that kind of person. You always look things up and check on them. I bet you were a straight-A student, weren't you?"

With his fingers sifting through my hair and his thumb brushing along my neck, I was terribly distracted. Goose bumps prickled on my skin and my channel clenched.

It didn't seem to matter whether it was rational, I wanted Jesse. Badly. In the back of my mind, a part of me was worried—worried that I was letting myself even think about this, that I was letting myself even act on this.

I tried to tell myself it was nothing more than lust. But no man before even came close to the way I felt about Jesse. There was also the reality I'd been practically living like a nun the last few years. During medical school, I'd been insanely busy. Then my sister got diagnosed with cancer, so that tied me up emotionally and logistically. In the midst of that, my father had a stroke. During my last year of residency, it felt as if everything fell apart. The only point of sanity in my life was my residency, and I'd buried myself in it. They died within six months of each other, my father going first and then my sister Karen. Sex hadn't even been on my radar.

I completely lost track of what Jesse said. Glancing up to him, I bit my lip. "I forgot what you said."

His eyes searched my face, his mouth hitching up at one corner. Oh geez, his grins were just dangerous. "I asked if you were a straight-A student in school," he murmured, sliding his hand down to cup the back of my neck.

I could feel his arousal at the apex of my thighs where he stood between my knees. I distantly knew he was asking about my grades—a rather pointless topic—and yet it felt as if an entirely separate conversation was happening between our bodies.

"I was," I finally managed to say, the second word coming out with a gasp when he slid his hand down my spine to cup my ass and rocked his arousal into me.

"I think I should go," he said.

"Why?"

My question just slipped out, and I suddenly wondered if I'd gotten this all wrong. I didn't know what expression he saw on my face, but he shook his head quickly.

"Don't be thinking now. The problem is I'm about this close—" he held up his thumb and forefinger with a tiny sliver of space between them — "to tearing your clothes off and bending you over this counter. But your mother's upstairs, and it doesn't feel quite right."

Oh, how I wanted to argue the point with him. Because his words sent a rush of need through me. I wanted to drag him to bed right now. I knew just as well as he likely did that my mom could wake up at any time. It wasn't that I needed her permission, or anything ridiculous like that. But, I'd rather her know about us instead of meandering down to the kitchen and finding us fucking each other.

"Oh," I managed, just before his palm swept up my spine. He laced his fingers into my hair and brought his mouth to mine. In a flash, his tongue was tangling with mine, and his palm was cupping my cheek. He kissed me as if he couldn't get enough, while I kissed him back as if he was the very air I needed to breathe.

In this moment, he was.

He pulled away far too quickly. I felt bereft when he drew back. He didn't step away, not just yet. His eyes coasted over mine.

What he said next startled the hell out of me.

"I like you, Charlie. I don't want you to think this is just about sex for me."

My mouth must've fallen open because he smiled. "I'm not a jerk. I think I've made that clear."

"Oh I don't think you're a jerk, I just didn't expect you to say that," I finally said. My thoughts whirred in my mind—a mix of desire, want, and uncertainty. This felt so, so good, and yet my life felt so, so messy. "My life is, um, kind of complicated."

"I noticed, but I don't give a damn."

When he stepped away, I literally had to hold myself back from following him. He smiled. "6 o'clock. I'll be here. Should I bring coffee?"

"Let's stop and get some at Firehouse Café."

"Perfect." At that, he spun away and winked just before he closed the door behind him.

Chapter Eleven

CHARLIE

The following morning, my mother and I were ready to go just a few minutes before 6 o'clock. My mother was beside herself to learn where we were going. I'd told her last night, but she'd forgotten. She had better and worse days. Today appeared to be one of the better ones so far. Her eyes were clear and she was on track.

When Jesse knocked on the door, she beat me to it, swinging it open and gracing him with a wide smile. "Good morning, Jesse. Are you ready?"

He flashed a grin. "Of course I'm ready. I'm here on time." Glancing to his watch, he caught my eyes when he looked up. "I'm actually three minutes early."

This delighted my mother. With a laugh, she spun around to grab her jacket off the coat rack.

Jesse glanced my way again. "You ready?"

"Of course. I wasn't sure if I should bring anything for lunch."

He shook his head. "I don't think so. There are plenty of places to eat there. We should be all set. I've got water in the truck."

Snagging my purse, I tucked a few of my mom's favorite snack bars in there, and then we were off. Within a few minutes, Jesse pulled up in front of Firehouse Café. I'd quickly grown to love this place after we first moved here. For starters, they had amazing coffee and baked goods. But it was Janet James, the owner, who made it one of the local favorites. She was warm and welcoming. She made me feel it was possible for us to eventually fit into the quirky little community of Willow Brook.

My mother walked in with us. She loved getting tea here. There was already a line, but then that was usually the case. 6 AM wasn't an unusual time for me to swing by here, not when I wanted to get to the office to do paperwork before my day started.

Jesse greeted a few people, as did I. While we were waiting in line, another firefighter, whom I'd met in passing when he injured his hand, paused to greet us on his way out. Beck Steele was roguish and handsome and always ready with a quip.

"Morning, Jesse," he said with a nod.

His eyes caught mine, and he reflexively winked. I imagined he winked at just about everyone—men and women alike. He proved my point by winking at my mother. Beyond his teasing, he only had eyes for his wife whom he clearly adored. I'd met Maisie when she'd come in with him the day he'd injured his hand. It had been one of my more amusing encounters. She'd bossed him the entire time, and I was pretty sure he loved it.

"Morning, Charlie," he offered.

"Good morning," I replied.

My mom looked over at him, gracing him with one of her sweet smiles. Beck smiled right back at her. "I don't think I've met you. I'm Beck Steele," he said, holding out his free hand.

My mother shook it and then winked at him. "I'm Olive, and you're a flirt," she announced.

Beck simply flashed a grin and shrugged, entirely unabashed. "Maybe so."

"We're going to the Bird Fest," my mother added. "Jesse's taking us."

I could see the curiosity in Beck's gaze, but he didn't say anything. Glancing to Jesse, he winked. "Well, the weather's on your side today. Have a nice drive and enjoy it." He started to turn away and then turned back, lifting his coffee cup. "Nice to meet you, Olive," he called.

My mom simply smiled. As we waited, I glanced around. The café occupied the town's original fire station. The old garage had been transformed with seating for dining and an open style bakery and kitchen. Brightly painted fireweed flowers decorated the old fire poles. The café had dashes of bright colors throughout with pink windowsills and the concrete flooring stained light blue. Small wooden tables were scattered through the dining area with a counter that offered more seating. The space was warm, inviting and cheerful, ideal during the long winter days.

When we reached the front of the line, Janet was there waiting. Her dark hair shot through with silver was pulled back into a braid. Her brown eyes crinkled at the corners with her smile when she saw us. "Well, good morning, Olive and Charlie."

When Jesse stepped to my side, a subtle gleam entered her gaze. I had no doubt Janet wouldn't hesitate to ask me about his presence with us at another time, but likely not now with my mother here.

"I'm covering everything," Jesse said, glancing to my mother. "What do you need, Olive?"

"Tea please," she replied, casting a warm smile at Jesse.

Janet looked to me next. "I'll take the house coffee today. Whatever you've got as long as it's strong."

"How about I add a shot of espresso just for good measure?" Janet asked. "You Jesse?"

"I'll take the same, but add two shots to mine."

With a smile and a wink, Janet spun away and started prepping our drinks. Jesse glanced down to me. "Anything to eat?" he asked, his tone low.

"Why don't we get some pinwheels? That should tide us over until lunch."

Jesse called over to Janet, "Do you mind heating up four of those pinwheels?"

"Of course not," she replied, not even looking over as she slid my mother's tea onto the counter.

When she handed over our coffees, Jesse paid, nearly glaring at me when I tried to offer to pay. We sidled out of the front of the line to wait for the pinwheels. One of the teens who helped Janet at the register came out front, and Janet leaned on the counter to chat with us while we waited. My mother had wandered over to the windows.

"So, how is she doing?" Janet asked.

Janet was sweet to my mom and always checked in on her. I shrugged, taking a sip of my coffee. "As well as could be expected, I suppose. She hasn't wandered off in the last two weeks."

"Well, I was thinking about her the other day. My friend, Norma, helps run one of the groups at the local nursing home. She doesn't have to be a resident to go spend the day there," Janet suggested gently.

I felt Jesse's gaze on me, but he stayed quiet.

"I don't know..." I started to say and then Janet narrowed her eyes, her gaze warm but somber.

"Hon, you can't do this all on your own. You've got a teenager and that's enough of a handful. Something to help you not worry so much would mean a lot. It's just a thought."

I knew she meant well. I really did appreciate it, but I supposed I was still struggling to realize that this was where things are headed. I took another sip of my coffee, savoring the bitterness. "Maybe I'll bring her by for a visit sometime next week and see how it goes. I'm not as stubborn as you think. It's just whenever I bring up things like this, she gets upset."

"How about you come here, and I'll go over with you?" Janet offered.

I knew Janet's presence would probably help, but I felt the tug of my internal resistance. I knew it wasn't rational, I knew I needed to let go, but I was having a hard time facing what was actually happening with my mother. When it came to her, my emotions were winning the battle against my intellect.

"Okay text me a day when it would work next week, and I'll make it happen," I replied, nearly forcing myself to speak.

My mother wandered back over to us. "Are we ready?" she asked.

"That we are," Jesse said just as Janet handed over a small bag with our pinwheels. "We're headed down to Diamond Creek for the Bird Fest for the day."

Janet smiled widely. "It's the perfect day for it. I want to hear all about it," she said to my mother just before we turned away.

Chapter Twelve

JESSE

Driving south along the Seward Highway and then along the Sterling Highway, I enjoyed my coffee and a relatively quiet drive. Charlie had warned me sometimes her mother could get on conversation loops, which I didn't mind actually. I also didn't mind quiet either.

The view was spectacular along the way. Olive oohed and ahhed a few times as we rounded the curves on Turnagain Arm. The narrow stretch of highway was stunningly gorgeous with mountains rising tall on either side and the sun coming up above them. The sky held lingering bursts of color from its arrival, a soft pink hue coloring the horizon.

Occasionally, Charlie or her mother asked questions about areas we were passing through. When we reached Diamond Creek, I pulled over at the lookout on the side of the highway. We climbed out and walked to the railing. The view spilled out in front of us. Kachemak Bay was one of Alaska's coastal jewels. Encircled by mountains, the deep blue water sparkled under the sun. Diamond Creek was one of several communities situated on the shores of the bay.

The highway dipped down into the small community.

From this vantage point, the elevation offered an absolutely stunning view of the town and the mountains surrounding it. An eagle flew above us, its distinct, screeching call carrying through the air.

Olive clapped her hands, turning to beam at us. The mountains across the bay were still covered in snow, tall against the bright blue sky. Charlie glanced to me. "Thanks for bringing us. I know I could've..." Her words trailed off when I shook my head.

"I offered to take you because I wanted to. Plus, I get bonus time with you."

Her cheeks flushed and she sighed, biting her lip. "Where do we go to see the birds?"

It so happened one of the largest shorebird migrations in the world occurred in coastal Alaska. Millions of shorebirds migrated from South America to Alaska to nest during the summer. In several communities along the Kenai Peninsula and other parts of coastal Alaska, there were bird watching festivals to celebrate the massive migration.

"We need to go to the beach," I replied, unable to keep from grinning when she smiled. With a chuckle, I continued. "Come on, we'll head down to the harbor. We can park there and see where to go."

What followed was simply a plain good morning. Olive was enchanted with the birds, and they were truly everywhere. The tiny birds coated the beaches, gathering in different areas and feeding in the shallow waters along the sand. We meandered along a boardwalk, which offered viewing points with mounted binoculars for people to watch the birds.

Somewhere along the way, I caught Charlie's hand in mine, surprised when she didn't nudge me away.

Olive was a friendly sort as I'd already discovered. She was happy to chat with other birdwatchers as we made our way along the beach. She took tons of pictures with her phone with Charlie helping her. We grabbed a bite to eat at a small café by the beach. After lunch, Olive was starting to look tired, but she insisted she wanted to take one more walk. She declared she needed to feel the sand under the soles of her shoes.

We walked along the beach, pausing to watch a raft of otters floating in the bay. A curious seal followed along as we walked, rising out of the water occasionally to survey the beach. We looped back when Charlie pointed out it was getting late in the afternoon. As we started to walk up the stairs from the beach onto the deck that led to the parking area, Olive stumbled and fell.

"Oh!" She appeared more startled than hurt.

Charlie had been coming up behind Olive. Her eyes met mine, wide with concern. "Are you okay, Mom?"

I stepped to Olive's side, leaning down to check on her. Although she still didn't seem upset about her fall, she wasn't moving.

"I'm fine," she said, waving us away. She tried to move and then grimaced. "Well, I thought I was fine."

Catching Charlie's concerned gaze, I said, "Let me see if I can carry her."

Charlie leaned over and quickly checked to make sure it was safe to lift her. Though I was a trained emergency responder, Charlie was the doctor, so I deferred to her. When she deduced it was safe to carry Olive, I lifted her carefully into my arms. She was light as a feather with her slight build.

I'd been to Diamond Creek before, so I knew where the hospital was. Once we got to my truck, I glanced to Charlie. "Your call. We can drive up to the hospital ourselves, or call for help. It's probably gonna take more time to wait, but it's up to you."

Charlie nodded quickly. "You drive. Let's just go."

Chapter Thirteen

CHARLIE

I paced back and forth in the waiting room. I couldn't believe what had happened. Mom seemed fine actually. If she was in pain, I couldn't see it, at least not substantially. She had seemed primarily uncomfortable when they wheeled her in to check her out.

I was debating whether I should call Em now, or wait until we had more information. Rationally, I knew it was best to wait, but my anxiety was whirring through my thoughts and muddling everything. Meanwhile, Jesse had gone to get some coffee for us from the cafeteria. What had started out as a really great day had ended with me a ball of anxiety and worry.

I felt Jesse approach from behind, turning just as he rested a hand between my shoulders, his touch sliding down my spine. "She's okay. Take it easy. Someone should be out with an update soon."

He handed me a cup of coffee. Just holding the cup in my hand and having his touch on me eased the tension bundling up inside of me.

"I can't believe this happened," I muttered before taking a quick sip of coffee. It was surprisingly good.

My eyes widened, and Jesse shrugged as he guided me over to sit in the chairs. "I know, it's really good."

"Yeah, this is the best hospital coffee I've ever had."

Jesse chuckled. "I was just surprised as you. It's better than decent." His arm rested across my shoulders once I settled in the chair, the weight of it relaxing me. "I know you're stressed about your mom's fall, but all signs point to something minor."

As a doctor, I knew he was right, but it was next to impossible to be objective about my own mother. When I cast my eyes to him with a sigh, he rubbed my shoulder. "Hey, she had a great day. My guess is she threw something with her hip, or something like that."

"I know, I know. I just get worried."

"Right, but maybe you can wait to decide how freaked out you should be?"

"Maybe," I murmured.

We sat quietly, sipping coffee and watching the activity around us. It wasn't long before a nurse came into the waiting area. "You're with Olive Lane, right?" she asked. She had a warm air to her with bright brown eyes, a slender build, and her brown hair twisted into a braid.

Standing, I nodded quickly. "Yes, is she okay?"

"She's fine. She has a hairline fracture in her hip. I'm guessing that's where she landed when she slipped and fell."

I absorbed her explanation, a mix of tension and relief clashing inside. On the one hand, this was manageable and common for someone my mother's age. On the other, I didn't want her to be in pain.

Jesse nodded. "Sounds about right."

"What is the doctor recommending?" I asked. Mostly, I knew she needed rest and limited mobility.

"It's a small fracture, and it's stable, so the doctor thinks bed rest and physical therapy will be enough. She would like to keep your mother for the night, just to monitor her and make sure she's not in too much pain. I understand from Olive that you all live in Willow Brook. We can schedule follow ups with the local doctor there…"

Jesse cut in. "That's her," he offered with a wink.

The nurse smiled. "Oh, well, that makes it easy. Anyway, our scheduler can still call your office to make sure everything is in place."

"That would be great. Dr. Johnson has been seeing her, so our receptionist will make sure everything's set up. Is there anything she needs tonight?"

The nurse shook her head. "I don't think so. The doctor gave her something for the pain, which doesn't seem too bad so far. She was worried that it would set in during the night. Seeing as it's getting late, she's already asleep. We can monitor her tonight and make sure nothing else is going on. Tomorrow, we'll do some blood work, get her fitted for a cane and send her home with a walker."

I felt myself nodding along. In a way, I was relieved. There was the obvious relief that a hip fracture was minor and fairly common at my mother's age. Recovery could be complicated, but for now, she was fine. I'd also been trying to persuade my mother for months to try a walker, but she'd been fighting me on it. A flash of guilt rose inside. I suddenly worried if I should've taken her on this day trip, no matter how much she'd wanted to come. With a hard shake, I forced my mind off that track. I couldn't turn back time.

The nurse's pager went off. "Any more questions?"

"I don't think so," I replied, spinning through a few logistical ones, but aware the nurse couldn't answer those for me.

"Would you like to check in on her? She's asleep, but if you want to see her, that's fine," the nurse said.

"Yes, that would be great," Jesse said, answering for me.

"She's in room 34. It's down the hall to the right." She hurried away with a quick wave.

Jesse caught my eyes. "Doing okay?"

I nodded. "Yeah. I have a few things to figure out at the house, but she's okay and that's all that matters."

He caught my hand in his and walked with me down to the room. My mother was sound asleep. She looked peaceful and comfortable, so the tension knotted inside loosened a little more. As we were standing by her bed, another nurse came in. She checked my mother's vitals, casting a smile our way. "Your mom is a funny one," she offered.

"Oh yeah?"

"Oh yes. I'm sure you're worried, but she's going to be fine. All she could talk about was what a great day she had seeing the birds. Slipping and falling is part of getting older, and she took it in stride."

I smiled, relief washing through me. "Is there anyone else I need to check in with before tomorrow?"

"Check in at the desk on your way out. They'll give you the schedule for the morning."

I dropped a kiss on my mother's forehead and then we left the room. After Jesse tossed his empty coffee cup in the wastebasket as we passed it by, he caught my hand in his. I loved the feeling of his grip—warm and strong. It was nice not to feel alone in this, not today. When we got in the truck, I glanced over at him. "I think I'll call Em now. I don't want her to worry."

"What would she be worried about? She doesn't even know anything happened," he said with a grin.

I rolled my eyes. "You're right. I suppose I'm projecting my worry onto her. But, we won't be home tonight, so I at least want her to know that. All in all, it's a good thing she's with a friend for the weekend."

I slipped my phone out of my purse to call when Jesse spoke. "Hey, quick question."

"What?"

"I'm thinking we should grab a hotel for the night. Okay with you if we head down to the harbor? There are a few hotels down there."

"Sounds like a plan."

I didn't let myself dwell on what it meant that I'd be spending the night in a hotel with Jesse. I started to ponder whether we'd share a room and immediately brought my thoughts to a screeching halt. I didn't need to obsess about this. Not now.

He started driving, and I called Em, wondering if she would even answer. I was surprised when she answered on the third ring. "Hey, Aunt Charlie, what's up? Checking up on me?"

"Don't you wish," I said, smiling to hear she was in a good mood.

"Actually I was just calling to let you know we won't be back until tomorrow. Gram had a little fall. She's fine, but she fractured her hip."

"Oh no! Is she okay?"

"She's going to be fine. They're keeping her for the night to make sure she's stable. Honestly, Em, I was worried at first, but she didn't even seem to be in a lot of pain. The only reason we knew something was wrong was when she couldn't quite get up."

"Oh," she said softly, quiet for a moment. "What should I do?"

"Nothing. You relax and we'll be home tomorrow."

"What are you and Jesse going to do?"

"We're staying at a hotel." The moment I spoke, I realized she might read into what that might mean. I hoped she could leave it be for now.

To my relief, she did. "Okay. Tell grandma I said hi, and I'll see her tomorrow, okay?"

After I tapped to end the call, I glanced to Jesse. "Well, that went well. She's had a rough year and she's close to my mom, so I didn't want her to worry."

He rolled to a stop at an intersection. "Yeah?"

His comment was vague enough that I didn't have to answer, but I figured I might as well.

"Her mom died of cancer. She was my sister. It was hard on all of us but, of course, it was hardest on Em. First, she had to watch her mom get sick and then she died. My dad also passed away about six months before, so..."

I swallowed through the emotion knotting in my throat. I didn't talk about it a lot because, well, I'd been busy simply picking up the pieces of my life and trying to carry on.

Jesse glanced over, his gaze understanding. After a beat, he spoke, "No wonder you walk around like you have the weight of the world on your shoulders. You're taking care of everyone. That can't be easy."

I held his gaze. The simple acknowledgment of what I'd been trying to manage somehow eased its weight. "Maybe not, but I wouldn't have it any other way."

He nodded slowly. The light changed to green, and he looked away. "Okay, here's the deal, I say we stay at Midnight Sun Lodges and go out for dinner. You're not allowed to worry. Your mom is in good hands, and she's comfortable. You get a free pass for tonight."

"Free pass?"

"You know, back when you were in school and got out of class for something. I know you love your mom, but you could use a break. She's where she needs to be, so you might as well relax."

I didn't quite know what to say to that, but my heart squeezed, and I wanted to cry again. I took a deep breath and let it out slowly. I wasn't quite ready to have an emotional meltdown in front of Jesse.

"Deal?" he asked.

"Deal," I replied, getting a grip on my emotions in the nick of time.

In short order, we'd checked in at Midnight Sun Lodges. Jesse didn't ask me if I wanted a separate room. I didn't, so I was relieved he didn't bother to ask. Just as I was about to ponder what I should wear tomorrow, Jesse pocketed the keycard to our room and turned to me.

"Okay, we need a change of clothes for tomorrow, so let's go shopping."

He drove into downtown Diamond Creek. The concept of "downtown" in Alaska was quite different than most places. Diamond Creek was small like Willow Brook, but it had even more tourist shops crowding the main street through town. Within moments, Jesse found a clothing shop. I purchased a T-shirt for the night and fresh set of clothes for tomorrow, figuring an extra pair of leggings and a sweatshirt would be put to plenty of use. He basically bought a repeat of what he was wearing—jeans and a black T-shirt.

Once we were back in his truck, he glanced over. "Okay, what do you like to eat?"

I was feeling a strange sense of giddiness. My worry for my mother was in the back of my mind, but for the moment I wasn't dwelling on it. It helped that I knew there wasn't anything I could do. She was resting comfortably with the nurse at the reception desk assuring me they'd call if anything changed.

I met his gaze and smiled. "I'll try anything."

"Not helping much," he said with a slow grin. "Let's see, there's the Boathouse, that's a little nicer than average with seafood. There's also Diamond Creek Brewery."

"What's that?"

"An actual brewery with a restaurant attached. The menu is casual, but they've got a bit of everything."

"Let's go there," I replied.

"Perfect. That's within walking distance, so I'll just leave my truck at the hotel."

We returned to the hotel, dropped off our purchases, and then walked hand in hand to Diamond Creek Brewery. Entering the restaurant, I glanced around. What was once an old plane hangar had been refurbished into a modern restaurant. The high-ceilinged space, which had enough space for two small planes, was now a restaurant and brewery. The brewery part of the business was to the back with the stainless steel brewing equipment visible behind a waist-high brick wall with two decorative copper storage vessels flanking the entrance into the brewery.

Model planes hung from the ceiling, most of them models of the small two to six-seater planes that crisscrossed the skies of Alaska. Windows had been added with most of the walls broken up with stunning views of an adjacent marshy field against a backdrop of the bay and mountains in the distance. Booths lined the walls and tables were scattered in the middle of the space. The kitchen was against the far wall with a bar currently crowded with customers. The cavernous space was softened with fabric wall hangings and colorful rugs.

Within minutes, we were seated at a booth. I selected one of the wines they made on site, while Jesse perused the beer selection for several minutes before settling on a seasonal winter beer. After our waiter left to get our drinks, Jesse leaned back in the booth, cocking his head to the side. "I think you should let your hair down," he said. The grin that followed sent desire curling through me.

I'd pulled it back into a ponytail this morning, thinking it would be windy and I didn't want to bother with it. I'd been right on both counts. It was breezy here by the ocean, and I never wanted to bother much with my hair. I felt my cheeks flush as I looked over at him. "I should?"

"I don't know if *should* is the right word. It's more that I love it when your hair is down."

For a moment, I just stared at him. Honestly, my hair wasn't something I thought much about. I simply didn't have time. The most time I'd spent on my appearance in the last few years was when Em had persuaded me to dye my hair with that streak of purple. It had been fun because she loved it. Every time it started to fade, she offered to do it again.

Reaching out, I tugged the elastic out of my hair and let it fall loose. The slow, devastating grin that stretched across

Jesse's face made my skin prickle and need coil in my core, radiating outward.

He didn't say anything else, but the heat in his eyes was enough. Our waiter arrived, delivering my gooseberry wine and Jesse's beer. Taking a sip, I glanced over at Jesse. "Oh my God. This is really good. I mostly got it out of curiosity."

He chuckled. "Yeah, they know what they're doing here. It's not just a hobby."

"It's pretty busy here," I observed as I glanced around at the mostly full tables and the line beginning to form at the entrance.

"It's like this most of the time here. It's another tourist destination. There's a ski lodge here too, so they stay busy all year long. Like Willow Brook, it's crazy in the summer. Give it another couple of months, and we'd have been waiting about a half an hour just to get a table here. Have you been through summer here yet?"

"We moved here right at the end of summer last year, so not really. I hear things get busy."

"They do. Alaska's on a lot of bucket lists. I'd say like you, but you were born here, so you're a true Alaskan," he offered with a wink.

I burst out laughing. "I don't quite buy that. I hardly remembered it."

Jesse shrugged. "Alaska has a lot of transplants. It's a bit of *thing* to be born here."

I leaned back, sipping my wine and eyeing him. "Were you born in Alaska? All I know so far is you grew up in Fairbanks and your family moved to Willow Brook after you graduated from high school. Oh and why did you become a firefighter?"

He drummed his fingers on the table. "I was born in Fairbanks. My parents ended up there for the same reason yours were outside of Anchorage. My dad was in the military and got stationed there. As for becoming a firefighter, well probably because I like being outside. I went to college and got a degree in geology because I liked being outside. But I realized that kind of work was mostly academic. Not really my thing. I signed on for my training one summer and loved it. I can't do it forever. It's pretty hard work physically, but I figure I'll do it as long as I can. I love the wilderness, and I like pushing myself to my limits physically. It also feels good to make sure people are safe."

"So you're on one of the hotshot crews, right?"

Since I worked at the only general medical clinic in Willow Brook, quite a few of the local firefighters passed through our office for minor injuries. I'd learned the Willow Brook Fire & Rescue housed two hotshot crews and a local crew. Due to its central location in Alaska, Willow Brook was a convenient point for travel.

Jesse nodded. "Yup. I'm foreman on one of the crews. During the winter, we're mostly in Willow Brook, but in the summers we'll be in and out of town whenever and wherever they need us. I've gotta be honest, my shoulder finally feels back to one-hundred percent. I know I complained about those extra two weeks, but I think it helped," he said.

I grinned. "Good. I really wasn't trying to give you a hard time. But you're not my patient anymore, so next time you might have better luck with Doc Johnson."

"Nah, he's a hard ass too," he replied with a chuckle. "Anyway, your turn. I know you were born in Anchorage when your father was stationed at Elmendorf, but not much else. How long were you here before your parents moved away?"

"I was five, so I don't remember much, just a few fuzzy memories."

"And then?" he prompted.

"Then, up until high school, my dad got stationed in different places. He was in the Air Force, so we were in North Carolina, in Texas, and overseas in Germany once. He retired after he was stationed in Massachusetts. We stayed just outside of Boston while we were there. I graduated from high school in Massachusetts, went to college and straight into med school. Then my sister, Emily's mom, was diagnosed with pancreatic cancer. That was just awful. We were ten years apart, and she was older. For my last two years of med school, we were all dealing with that. She was going to doctors, getting chemo, and everything. Em was having a hard time. Her dad hasn't exactly been around. Ever. Then, my dad had a stroke. That was just one more thing. He ended up dying of complications. This sounds weird, and I don't mean it to be weird, but in a way, it would've been easier on my mom if he just died right away. Instead, she got hopeful. And who wouldn't? We all got hopeful. But he never bounced back. She had to make all these awful decisions. Meanwhile, my sister Karen was dying. Inside of six months, they both died. Even though I knew Mom's memory was starting to go, it wasn't like it is now. So we decided to move. I wanted to give her the one thing that she had missed for so many years. Plus, I thought a fresh start somewhere new might be good for all of us. We got here, and her memory slide sped up. And..."

I ran out of words for a moment. When I paused, Jesse nodded, his gaze somber, still just listening.

"So here we are. I'm a parent in the legal sense of the word and trying to be pretty decent at it, but half the time I don't know what the hell I'm doing. I feel guilty because Em's mom died and her dad was never around. I worry it's too much on her to watch my mom slowly go too."

I recited the series of events quickly, all of the emotion of those years void in my words. It wasn't gone inside, but the telling of it was distant because I couldn't handle anything else. Jesse didn't say anything, so I continued, letting it all out in a rush. "Right before my sister died, she didn't want me to just have guardianship of Emily because those could be overturned more easily. So she set it up for me to adopt Emily once she knew she was dying. Em's dad isn't the greatest guy. If my sister hadn't gotten pregnant, I doubt she'd have seen him again. I figured he might fight her on the adoption, but he didn't even bother to come to court. So all that happened. Like I told you, my mother always wanted to come back to Alaska, so I decided we should try moving. I figured we could use a fresh start. Only I didn't count on her memory slipping so quickly."

Jesse was quiet for a few moments. I sipped my wine, thinking I could use something to take the edge off. It felt funny to be here, almost as if this was an actual date. Yet, there was no way to talk about my life without its inherent messiness spilling out. If I spent much time on social media, I'd have had an entirely depressing string of posts unless I lied through my teeth.

He opened his mouth to say something when our food arrived. I'd gotten halibut tacos, and he gotten some kind of king crab dish. The interruption was welcome. I hadn't quite meant to dump out the last few years of my life all at once like that. But then, it just showed how out of practice I was with this. I didn't seem to know how to gloss over any of it.

Once we were settled and eating, he caught my eyes again. "I know you worry about your mom, but I think it's probably good you're here. Willow Brook's a lot smaller than Boston, but once you line up some help for her when you're at work, you won't have to worry. I don't know if you could have given her a better gift than bringing her to the place she always said she wanted to return."

His tone was light, yet my heart gave a hard thump at his words. I'd spent a lot of time doubting just about every decision I'd made in the last year or so. The only decision I hadn't questioned was adopting Em. There had been no need to even contemplate that. The moment my sister asked me, I'd known the answer. I'd already loved Em to pieces. No matter how unprepared I felt at times, there was no doubt for me. Yet, it had still been hard to pick up the reins. Layering atop that was the grief for my father and sister and the sharp pain at witnessing my mother slide slowly into confusion.

I took a bite of my food, savoring the rich halibut, before sipping my wine. I needed a moment to gather myself. I wasn't usually too emotional, but Jesse had a strange effect on me. On the heels of a deep breath, I opted to keep a light tone.

"Do you mean you don't think we should plan for Waffle to watch guard over my mom?"

He flashed a grin, his low chuckle sending a shiver down my spine. "That's a back up for emergencies only. It's not really a plan. I get the sense you already know this, but even if your mom puts up a fight, I think once you have somebody set up to help her, she'll settle right in."

I took a deep breath, letting it out with a sigh before taking a sip of my wine. "I think you're right," I said softly. "I'm getting there."

The rest of dinner passed uneventfully. Well, I mean, if you didn't count the fact this was the closest thing I'd had to a date since college. It was more of an accidental date. Yet, with Jesse sitting across from me, looking ridiculously handsome with his tousled amber hair and his knowing green gaze, desire spun through my veins the entire time.

By some miracle, I really didn't dwell on worrying about my mother. She was safe and sound, and we'd see her in the morning. I felt like I could put my worries on the shelf in a closet and close the door for the night. So that was exactly what I did.

Chapter Fourteen

JESSE

Charlie sat across from me, her cheeks flushed, the tension gone from her face, and her gorgeous hair falling down around her shoulders. Meanwhile, all I could think about was getting her back to the hotel and getting her bare naked.

But I was a gentleman. I managed to get through dinner. I didn't go all caveman and throw her over my shoulder on the way out. I caught her hand in mine, and we walked back to the hotel in the late evening.

The air was cool with a salty breeze gusting off the bay. The evening was quiet with the sound of waves rolling into the shore and seagulls calling in the distance. When we got to the hotel, once we were in the elevator, I glanced over to Charlie. Our eyes collided, and it was as if a flame spun to life, heating the air around us.

I didn't even hesitate. With her hand still held in mind, I stepped in her direction as I tugged her to me. We came together with a soft bump. Her hand slid up to cup the back up my neck, and she leaned up to kiss me. I couldn't have said who kissed whom first.

All I knew was the moment my lips met hers that flame

flashed hot around us, catching us in its center. In a matter of seconds, her tongue was tangling with mine, and she was arching into me. She was cool and smelled crisp like the air outside.

I didn't even notice the elevator coming to a stop until the sound of the doors swooshing open nudged my consciousness. Drawing away, I caught her eyes. Her gaze was smoky, and her lips were swollen from our kiss. It was a damned good thing I had a loose grip on my control. Otherwise, I would've taken her right there in the elevator.

Instead, catching her hand in mine again, I tugged her out of the elevator, and we practically ran down the hall. Fumbling for the keycard, I got us in the room and then spun around.

We collided against the door, tearing at each other's clothes. Charlie all but climbed my body, her legs curling around my hips as I lifted her up against me. Her head thumped against the door when I tore my lips free, needing to taste her skin.

The thump nudged me out of my haze, and I lifted my head. "You okay?"

Charlie's eyes were wild, lightning flashing in the silvery gray when she opened them. "Uh huh," she murmured.

She slid her palm down my chest and curled it over my cock, which was straining against my fly. I groaned, murmuring her name. Dipping my head, I moved to kiss her again, but she shimmied down, spinning me around quickly. Then, she was on her knees in front of me, looking up at me through her thick dark lashes as she deftly undid the buttons on my fly. My cock sprang free from my briefs, so hard it ached. Leaning forward, she dragged her tongue along the underside, catching the drop of pre-cum on the tip.

"Fuck, Charlie," I growled.

She laughed softly, the sound tightening the need already coiling inside of me. With her eyes on mine, she leaned forward again, curling her fist around the base of my cock.

Sliding my hand down, because I needed something to hold onto, I laced my hand in her hair, watching as she proceeded to drive me out of my fucking mind.

Another swipe of her tongue, and then she took me into the warm, slick heat of her mouth. Loosely gripping my shaft, her fist slid up and down as she drew me inside again and again. Sensation gripped me, the claws of need scoring me deeply. Yet, this wasn't how I wanted to let go, not right now. Grasping onto the reins of my control, just barely, but enough to slow the thundering need pounding through me and almost cresting to a wave.

"Charlie," I bit out.

She paused, leaning back and dragging her tongue across her bottom lip. She was so fucking sexy with her hair falling down, her cheeks flushed, and her lips damp and puffy.

I didn't know what the hell I meant to say. But since I couldn't seem to form another word, I reached down and lifted her up against me. In two strides, we reached the bed. I tugged her shirt up over her head. She got with the program quickly, shimmying out of her leggings as I threw my shirt to the floor and kicked my jeans free. Somewhere along the way, we tumbled onto the bed.

Her skin was soft and silky against mine as she shifted and flexed into me. I was angled half over her with my leg resting between her thighs. Her breasts pushed against my chest as I kissed her as if my life depended on it, as if I couldn't breathe without her. I was more accustomed to being able to have some finesse. But with Charlie, there was no finesse—everything was raw and primal.

I needed to taste her. Catching her lips in another drugging kiss, I drew back slowly, dusting kisses along the side of her neck and down across her breasts. Teasing her nipples with my thumb, I savored her husky cries.

Mapping my way down her body, I glanced up, my cock hardening even further at the sight of her. Her hair was spread out over the pillows, a wild, dark tangled mess. Her skin was flushed and dewy.

Dipping my head again, I kissed my way over the soft curve of her belly, trailing my fingers through her folds. She was hot and slick. I sank a finger into her channel before dragging my tongue across her seam. She tasted salty and sweet. Everything I wanted. Gripping her hip with one hand, I teased her with my fingers as I settled in to drive her wild.

With her husky cries and her hips bucking into my mouth, she was at the edge sooner than I expected. I wanted to savor this. I loved seeing her fly apart. The uptight oh-so-professional woman I'd come to know had a wild side, and it drove me right to the edge of my control. Layering into that was the reality that the more I got to know her, to understand the person she was underneath, the more I wanted her to let go in more ways than one.

She cried out, her channel clamping down around my fingers when I swirled my tongue over her clit, sucking it lightly into my mouth. I didn't wait. I was too close to my own edge. Rising up, I mapped my way back up over her body, settling my hips into the cradle of hers. Her slick heat called to me as she curled her legs around me.

At the absolute last second, I remembered I didn't have a condom on.

"Fuck," I muttered, rolling off of her swiftly.

She followed my motion, straddling me on top. "Where are you going?" she murmured, her voice husky and fierce.

Looking up at her with her hair tousled around her shoulders, her skin flushed and her lips swollen, I gritted my teeth and held onto my control. It was taking everything I had not to bury myself inside of her with the slick folds of her pussy teasing over my cock.

"Condom," I bit out.

Her eyes widened, and she held still, staring at me for a moment. "I have an IUD," she finally said. "Not because I was planning on this, but I'm a doctor. I'm practical like that."

Her cheeks flushed a deeper shade of pink, uncertainty flickering in her eyes.

"Are you sure?" I asked.

"I'm clean. I haven't been with anyone other than you in over three years. I trust you would say something if I needed to be concerned."

"Of course I would, but this is your call, not mine."

"In that case..." she murmured, her lips curling in a sly grin.

She rose up between us, gripping my cock and shifting her hips to draw me into her creamy clench, inch by inch. It was pure heaven.

"There," she said softly once she was seated with me buried to the hilt inside of her.

Staring up at her with her hair falling around her shoulders and her eyes flashing like lightning, my heart thudded hard and fast. She was glorious, so damn beautiful and sexy, my breath caught in my throat.

I knew this wasn't simply desire. Every moment with her was so powerful, the physical connection spinning into a shimmering web of intimacy, binding us tighter and tighter together.

Then, she started to move. Gripping her hips, I let her set the pace as she rose up and sank down, rocking into me. Everything blurred into sensation, need scoring through me deeply with every stroke.

Chapter Fifteen

CHARLIE

"Charlie..." Jesse murmured my name, his voice husky, curling around my heart.

Dragging my eyes open, I met his gaze just as he reached between us, his thumb pressing over my clit. That was all it took as he surged into me again. Pleasure spun tightly and then let loose, fiery sparks scattering through me as I cried out, my channel clenching around him. Falling against him, his hoarse cry reverberated through me as he went rigid, the heat of his release pouring into me.

His palm slid up my back, holding me close. We lay still, our breath the only sound in the quiet room, rough and ragged. His skin was damp, as was mine. With my cheek resting against his chest, I listened to the sound of his heart beating along with mine.

After a few minutes, I lifted myself up, resting my chin on my hand. His eyes opened, a slow smile stretching across his face. A rush of emotion rose inside. A smile tugged at the corners of my mouth. It felt that good to be with him. I was relaxed to my bones, relaxed in a way I hadn't been in years. When life was busy and hard things happened, your baseline became one of worry and tension and you almost forgot what it was like to let those things go, even temporarily.

"I get you for the night," he murmured softly, his hand sliding up my spine to sift through my hair.

"You do," I replied, thinking how sublime it was.

On the heels of that, the recollection of my usual life flashed in my mind. There were so many reasons why it didn't make sense for me to contemplate romance.

Whether he was reading my mind or not, Jesse immediately honed in on the direction of my thoughts. "There's nothing to worry about right now. Your mom is fine. Emily's probably having a great time at Kayla's too," he offered.

I took a deep breath, letting it out in the shuddering sigh. "I know, I'm not quite used to not worrying."

"I noticed."

He didn't say anything else for a moment, and I thought maybe the topic would just drop. But no.

"I know the last few years have been pretty rough." I sensed he was asking a question, even though his words came out as a statement.

"Um, yeah, it's been a rough couple of years. This would be the part where you stay quiet, but think to yourself that you'd better run the minute you get the chance," I said with a laugh, thinking back to everything I'd dumped on him during dinner.

It wasn't even a bitter laugh. What I didn't say aloud was that I would deal with it when that happened because I figured it was inevitable. It would be hard, harder than I'd anticipated though.

Jesse's eyes searched mine. "Sweetheart, I knew your life was complicated from the start, even when I thought you were uptight as hell. I'm not gonna go running just because of that though."

I didn't quite know what to think of that. Yet, I couldn't help the curl of warmth that squeezed my heart. I had no idea how to fit Jesse into my life, but it seemed to be happening.

"Okay," I finally said, uncertain what else to say.

"If you don't mind me asking, what's the deal with Emily's dad?"

I took another deep breath because no matter how you sliced it, it was depressing.

"Well, you know how I said her mom was ten years older than me?" At his nod, I continued. "She got pregnant when she was a freshman in college. It definitely wasn't planned. I don't even like calling him Em's dad because he's never been there for her. He was just a sperm donor, some guy my sister met at a party. When she told him she was pregnant, I don't think he gave a damn one way or another. His only question was whether or not she was going to have an abortion. She thought about it, but she decided against it because she really wanted to have the baby. So she did. I'm sad for Em that he's never been around. He's never paid a dime in child support, never really been involved. Every so often, he calls Em. He used to show up and badger my sister for money. I was worried I'd have to deal with him after my sister died. But when she knew she was dying, and she knew it was a sure thing, she filed the paperwork for the adoption to go through upon her death. She didn't want me to have to worry about him trying to appeal a guardianship later. He didn't even contest it, especially when I agreed in advance to never seek child support from him. It still broke Em's heart."

Jesse was quiet. "Fucking asshole," he muttered.

I laughed, if only because that was the plain truth. "Yeah. Fucking asshole."

"So you adopted her?"

"I did. My sister really wanted it. There was never any question for me that I'd take care of Em, but I wanted it to be her choice. I don't ever expect her to call me Mom because I'm her aunt."

"You're a good mom," Jesse said, his fingers still sliding through my hair, almost lulling me.

"Do you think?" I asked, looking up at him.

He grinned, promptly managing to send flutters spinning through my belly. Dear God. I wondered if my need for him would ever be slaked.

"Yes, I think. No matter how cranky she might be with you, she's a good kid. After everything she's been through, having you makes her pretty damn lucky."

Chapter Sixteen

JESSE

The following morning, I woke with Charlie, sweet, sexy Charlie, curled up beside me with her bottom nestled against my cock. My cock, by the way, was quite aware of the feel of her lush curves. She was warm, soft, and pure heaven to wake up beside.

My head was buried against the back of her neck. I took a deep breath, savoring her scent—musky with a hint of lavender. My hands started their own exploration, sliding down over her arm, into the dip of her waist, over the curve of her hip, and then angling over her soft belly to cup one of her breasts.

I grinned when her nipple puckered under the brush of my thumb. I couldn't resist tasting her, dipping my head to drop kisses along the side of her neck, my body tightening in response to the unconscious shiver that ran through her.

I felt when she came awake, her body tensing slightly and then a gasp escaping when I rolled her nipple between my thumb and forefinger, squeezing it lightly.

"Morning," I murmured in between kisses.

She shifted her legs restlessly, the motion brushing her

bottom against my cock, which swelled even further in response.

"Jesse," she murmured on a gasp when I nipped lightly along her neck as I slid my hand down over the soft curve of her belly to dip between her thighs. I found her hot, wet, and ready. Her hips arched into me. I shifted her leg, lifting it just enough to guide myself home inside of her.

Everything felt half awake, sleepy, languid, and sensuous.

We rocked together slowly, her snug channel clenching around me with every surge going deeper into her. Teasing my fingers over her clit, I circled until I felt her tighten and cry out. I followed her over, pleasure coiling tight and then snapping loose inside of me, crashing through me in a wave.

We lay still with me curled around her and buried deep inside of her for several long moments. I found I didn't want to get up. I could've stayed there all day.

Reality intruded in the form of Charlie's cell phone buzzing on the dresser. She turned, catching my eyes from behind, a sleepy half-smile on her face. "I'm guessing that's either Em, or the hospital."

"I'm guessing you're right," I replied, catching her lips in a quick kiss before I slowly drew out of her.

She stood from the bed and walked across the room to check her phone, completely bare, probably giving me the first moment to simply absorb the sight of her.

Her lush curves that were so well hidden when she was at work, tucked into her white lab coat, drew my eyes. I loved that she wasn't too thin.

She answered the call, mostly saying, *"Uh huh, okay"* and ending with, *"What time should we come?"*

That cued me it must be the hospital. I rolled out of bed and headed for the bathroom.

Chapter Seventeen

CHARLIE

After I checked in with the hospital and confirmed that we could pick my mother up for discharge around noon, I followed Jesse into the shower. I was discovering there was no environment where I didn't get hot and bothered when he was near.

Stepping into the steamy shower, I found Jesse leaning back under the water, rinsing soap out of his hair. The moment I saw him, my body tightened. It didn't even matter he'd just sent me flying once already this morning.

I sternly ordered my body to behave. Pulling the curtain closed behind me, I reached for the soap. When Jesse heard me, he opened his eyes, his mouth hitching at one corner.

"What's the news from the hospital?" he asked.

"Oh, they said my mom's doing fine. She'll be cleared for discharge by noon."

His eyes narrowed as he stepped out of the way for me to get under the water. "Isn't that kind of late? Is everything okay?"

"Discharge times are based on when they can process all the admin stuff. They wouldn't tell me she was ready for discharge if she wasn't actually ready. They said she slept well, and she's chatting with another patient who checked in late last night. I figure maybe we can grab some breakfast somewhere and then we'll go up there. They scheduled her with the lab for some routine blood tests. At her age, it's probably a good idea."

Jesse leaned against the tile and nodded, the concern fading from his gaze. "Sounds good. I'm glad she got some rest."

As I was rinsing the soap off my body, his gaze meandered down my body. He was grinning when his eyes made their way back to mine. I felt my cheeks flush as I lathered shampoo in my hair.

Unabashed, he flashed a grin and stepped out of the shower.

With hot water pouring down over me as I rinsed the shampoo away, I sighed. I worried I was getting in over my head.

As I stepped out of the shower to find him by the sink, he handed me a towel. I had to remind myself yet again that I couldn't just keep lusting after him. Yet, Jesse with a towel low on his hips, his muscled chest damp from the shower, and the subtle shadow of his beard were almost too much for me to resist. I managed, but just barely.

Not much later, we were both dressed and checked out of the hotel.

"Do you know anywhere to go for breakfast? You seem familiar with the area," I commented as I settled into the passenger's seat in his truck.

He glanced over. "I usually come fishing here a few times every summer. It's a great spot. When the weather's warmer, we should come for a few days."

I found myself nodding, and then considered the meaning of his comment—the implication that would be something we would do, like a couple.

Uncertain quite what to think about that, I asked, "So any suggestions for good coffee and breakfast?"

"Misty Mountain Coffee. They've got great coffee, and they serve breakfast."

"Then let's go."

At my nod, he started his truck and headed back into downtown Diamond Creek. Everywhere I looked, there were mountains and the ocean. The small town was nestled against the feet of the mountains with Kachemak Bay spilling out to the other side. A few minutes later, we were walking into Misty Mountain Café. The coffee shop was in a refurbished Quonset hut. The space was open and airy. They'd modernized the inside with finished walls and decorative timber beams crisscrossing the high ceiling. Brightly colored curtains and tablecloths made the space feel warm and playful.

The café was busy, and we filed into the back of the line at the counter. There was a warm and inviting quality to the place. After we ordered our coffees, we snagged a table that opened up by the windows. Taking a sip of my coffee, I sighed as I looked over at Jesse. "I love coffee. It's what got me through med school."

"I'm a fan myself. It gets me through every damn day," he replied with a grin.

We were quiet for a few moments. I looked around the café and wondered what it would be like for whatever was happening with Jesse to be more than the mirage it felt like. I'd felt as if I were suspended in time this entire weekend.

Then again, with last night feeling sort of like a date even though it was accidental, this morning made it feel even more as though we were something other than a passing encounter.

After we ate, we headed up to the hospital. We arrived at my mother's room just as she was about to be wheeled down to get her blood work done.

When she saw Jesse, she smiled widely. "Jesse! You're still here."

He grinned and winked, hooking a hand in his pocket as he looked down at her where she sat in a wheelchair. "Of course I am. Where'd you think I went? I get to take you home today."

My mother laughed, clearly delighted by his answer. The nurse who was wheeling her looked over to us. "Olive's done well. Aside from sleeping, she chatted with anybody who came by."

"How are you feeling, Mom?"

She looked over at me and shrugged. "I'm okay. They tell me I have to use a walker."

"That's what I hear," I offered, nodding and wondering if I should say anything else.

The nurse, as if though she read my mind, squeezed my mother's shoulder. "Hon, we just talked about this. You need to be stable on your feet, so that's the deal." At that, the nurse glanced at me and winked. "We're headed down to the lab if you to want to come with us," she offered.

"Sounds like a plan," I said, following along.

We were on the third floor of the hospital. The nurse led us to the second floor and down a long hallway. It didn't seem to matter where a hospital was, they all tended to feel the same—muted colors, bright lights, and a sense of hurry. Always clean, so clean it felt cold and sterile—the way it needed to be to remain that clean.

The nurse left us in the waiting room outside the lab. I couldn't go to a lab without thinking about my sister. The chemo area where she went at the hospital back in Boston was right beside the lab. She'd often shuttled back and forth between the two places getting things checked. I gave myself a shake, reminding myself there was nothing I could do about her death. I only hoped I had a little more time with my mom where she felt well and comfortable.

"Olive?" a voice called.

We all looked up to see a woman standing in the doorway to the waiting area. I instantly liked her. She had almost-black hair pulled up into a ponytail atop her head and translucent blue eyes. She wore a fluorescent green scrub top with pink stripes and a matching pink ribbon holding her hair up. Her wide smile was impossible not to return.

"That's me," my mother announced from her wheelchair.

Jesse stood and curled his hands on the handles, immediately wheeling her over to the woman. She looked down at my mother and held her hand out. "I'm Violet, nice to meet you."

"I'm Olive, and it's very nice to meet you," my mother returned.

I was discovering one upside to my mother's memory issues was her mood was generally cheerful. The only time she got irritable was when we discussed any changes, such as the walker and getting help at the house.

Violet glanced between us. "Are you here for moral support?"

"Up to you, Mom. Want company?"

My mom looked from Violet to Jesse to me and shrugged. "Well, they might as well come."

Violet grinned. "Follow me."

We followed her down a short hallway into a small room. Violet cocked her head to the side and reviewed the paperwork on her clipboard. "It looks like we're just doing the basics today. Okay, Olive, tell me which arm you prefer. Right or left?"

"I get to choose?" my mother asked.

"You sure do. As long as there's a good vein, it's up to you. Some people prefer I draw blood from their non-dominant arm. Although some people prefer to use their dominant arm because the pain goes away quicker when they use it a lot. I'm gonna be blunt here and say, at your age, let's pick whichever arm you use less."

Violet graciously listened as my mom regaled her with

stories of seeing the birds yesterday. I was beyond relieved that she seemed to remember most of the day. I was finding she had more challenges with remembering less recent events.

Violet teased her, and they joked about a few things. When she was done, we all walked down the hall together with Jesse wheeling my mother. Violet lightly tugged on my sleeve just as we reached the doorway to the waiting area.

"Just a quick question," she said.

Jesse took the cue and headed through the door to the waiting area.

Violet eyed me for a moment. "I know it's none of my business, and you'll probably never see me again, but do yourself a favor and find some help for your mom. She's a total sweetheart, and I can tell you're worried. The nurse told me that your mom says she doesn't need any help during the day. But I can guess she could probably use some company."

I hadn't known Violet for more than the perhaps ten minutes we'd been here. Yet, somehow the way she said this to me, I could handle it.

I swallowed and sighed. "I know. I'm working on it."

I was, but my intellect and reason kept bumping up against my emotions. This was hard, harder than I'd imagined. I didn't like watching my mother's memory slowly go and kept trying to convince myself she'd bounce back, even though I knew rationally she wouldn't. I was a doctor for crying out loud. I *knew* what was happening, but it didn't change the pangs of grief and the struggle to face the reality of it.

Violet's gaze was warm and understanding. "Okay, if that was totally inappropriate, just complain to my boss. She knows I tend to tell people what I think."

"Oh, you mean just offering your opinion when people might need to hear it?" I asked with a grin.

Violet smiled ruefully and shrugged. "Yes, that. Anyway, it was nice to meet you."

"Ditto."

Her pager went off. "Hey, Violet," I called as she reached to check it.

She glanced back to me.

"Thanks."

At her wide smile, I turned and went into the waiting room to meet Jesse and my mom. He arched a brow, an unspoken question in his eyes. I mouthed, "*All good.*"

Chapter Eighteen

JESSE

A few days later, I sighed as I leaned my hands against the tile in the shower at the station. We'd had a tough afternoon. There'd been a fire in a nearby town where multiple crews had been called from surrounding areas because it was big and out of control. A massive old mining building had caught fire. Unfortunately, a man had been exploring in there and had gotten trapped. We got the fire out, but he died from smoke inhalation before we could reach the area where he was trapped.

It didn't matter what I told myself, it hurt to lose someone. I let the pounding, steaming hot water wash away the day. I was physically exhausted and emotionally weary. As I dressed with a few of the other guys alongside of me, we were all quiet. I sat down on the bench, snagging a water bottle from my locker and draining it. When I tossed it into the recycle bin in the corner, Ward came walking into the locker room.

He leaned against the lockers across from Caleb and me. Caleb and I shared foreman duties on Ward's crew.

"We did all we could guys. Before we even got called out, it was probably too late," Ward said, his voice low.

"I know, man, but it still sucks," I replied, running a hand through my hair with a sigh.

What got to me the most was if we had been able to get there in time, we could've saved the man. By no means was this the first fatality that I'd dealt with as a hotshot firefighter over ten years. I'd even experienced the death of a crewmember who'd gotten trapped during a wildfire. That had been awful. In this case, the man had been in the back part of the mine, trapped behind the fire in the front section of the building. Every death weighed on me.

"Yeah, it sucks no matter what," Caleb said bluntly.

Ward sighed and nodded slowly. "I know. All we can do is what we can do.

We still have the weekend duty. Either one of you need to call out?"

"Nah, I'm good," I replied with Caleb nodding along with me.

He and I tended to approach these things in the same way, both of us preferring to throw ourselves back into the job.

As I drove towards home, all I could think was I wanted to see Charlie. In fact, I would've given just about anything to fall asleep with her tonight. When I turned onto my road, I started to go down my driveway and then stopped. I wanted, no *needed*, to see Charlie. Slipping my phone out, I sent a quick text.

Thought I'd stop by. Pizza?

I drove the remaining way down my driveway and stopped to feed Waffle before loading her up in the truck. Returning to town, I picked up three pizzas. I hadn't even waited for Charlie's reply, but I was relieved when it came in.

Sure. Em's kind of in a mood. She would probably love some pizza.

Despite my heavy day, just the knowledge that I was

going to see Charlie lifted the weight slightly. Waffle was, of course, excited. She was happy to go anywhere.

Within minutes, I was rolling around the circle at the end of their driveway. After a quick knock, Charlie opened the door. Waffle dashed through, and I glanced to Charlie. With Em as our audience, it was a good thing my hands were full with three pizza boxes. Without that, I didn't know if I could've kept myself from pulling Charlie into my arms.

I just needed her presence.

"Come on in," she said, gesturing as she stepped back.

Waffle was already playing on the floor with Emily. Stepping through, I glanced over to see Olive at the kitchen table, sound asleep in her chair.

"You could've told me your mom was asleep," I said, keeping my voice low as I followed her across the room.

Charlie cast a smile over her shoulder as she walked ahead of me toward the kitchen. "It's okay. She sleeps a lot. She could've been awake when you got here and fallen asleep halfway through dinner."

Charlie got plates out, handed me a beer, and poured herself a glass of wine before we slid onto the stools by the island counter. She caught my eyes and lowered her voice. "Normally, I'd ask Em to come eat with us, but I'll leave her be. I think something happened at school today because she's been cranky ever since she got home. Not that she's ever a ball of sunshine. I want to tell her she can talk to me, but I know the last person she wants to talk to is me. I feel like I can't win sometimes, but then I worry."

"Giving her space is probably a good call. I'll see if she wants some pizza though because I brought her favorite. That veggie deluxe thing she liked so much."

It wasn't a big deal to get the pizza Emily liked, but Charlie's smile made me feel like I'd just done the most amazing thing ever. That was how far this woman had nudged her way into my heart. It wasn't as if I'd been avoiding relationships before. I didn't even have an awful break-up story in my history. Yet, I wasn't accustomed to having someone matter this much.

Charlie had said it herself, but her life was most definitely complicated. It was funny how I didn't mind those complications at all. With her, they didn't feel like complications. They were simply part of her life. It never crossed my mind to back off.

Glancing over my shoulder, I called over to Emily. When she looked up, I asked, "You want some pizza? Got your favorite."

I'd spent enough time around my own niece these days to know how things tended to ebb and flow. There were good days and bad days. Just as Charlie had indicated, today appeared to be on the not-so-great side for Emily. She had always been nothing but polite to me. Yet, tonight she had a sullen look on her face. She was quiet for beat, her hand buried in the thick fur at Waffle's neck.

"I guess so," she finally said with a put-upon sigh. It sounded as if eating dinner was a burden.

I bit back my grin. I knew that sure as hell would not help matters, but teenage angst was amusing sometimes, especially when it was over something as simple as food.

Charlie caught my eye and the barest hint of a smile curled the corners of her lips. "Thank you," she mouthed.

Olive slept straight through dinner, while I wrestled with the wish to fall asleep beside Charlie tonight. Yet, we weren't on that footing just yet.

When we were cleaning up, Emily muttered something under her breath when Charlie asked her to bring her plate over to the sink. Charlie turned around, her eyes narrowing. Dishtowel in hand, she rested her hand on her hip and looked over at Emily. "Emily, it's obvious you're not in the best mood tonight. You've been rude to everyone. But the least you can do is bring your plate over," she said firmly.

Emily stomped over to the kitchen and all but flung her

plate in the sink. I heard the sound of it breaking as it hit the bottom of the sink.

"Hey..." I started to say, snapping my mouth shut when I realized it wasn't my place.

Emily glanced over at me, throwing a glare my way. Before she had a chance to say anything, Charlie cut in. "Emily, you just broke your plate. That's not okay."

Emily promptly burst into tears, looked at Charlie and said, "Well, Jesse's more important to you anyway. Just like everybody is."

With that, she stalked away, running up the stairs and slamming her door hard enough to for us to feel the vibration of it downstairs.

Charlie looked stricken. Her face was white, and a tear rolled down her cheek. "I can't believe she said that. Why would she feel like that?"

"Hey, I doubt she really feels like that, but she's upset right now. People say shitty things when they're upset."

I stepped to her, pulling her into my arms. She stiffened for moment and then relaxed against me, her forehead falling with a thump against my chest. "I know you're right, but it sucks. I need to go talk to her, okay?"

"Of course," I said, running my hand through her hair and down her back. My day was forgotten. Because all I wanted to do right now was to make her feel better. I sensed she was going to want me to leave. Even if I understood why, it didn't mean I liked it.

She stepped back, catching my hand to give it a squeeze. "Thanks for the pizza. Sorry my mom didn't wake up. She loves when you visit, you know."

I smiled. "I imagine she likes company in general. I'll go. I know you want to talk to Emily."

Charlie walked me to the door, stepping outside with me and closing it quietly behind her. It was late evening with the sky in that in-between place of light and dark. In the gloaming, Charlie's eyes were bright, an intensity contained within them. She leaned toward me just as I dipped down to her. Her hand slid into my hair at the back of my neck, and she brought her lips to mine softly.

I sighed, pulling her close because I needed her against me, to absorb the feel of her. Our kiss started soft—a brushing point of contact. The point of connection was electric—a hot jolt with flames flashing high in its wake.

Our kiss instantly became hot, deep, and intense, but it was more about emotion than desire. I was still reverberating from losing someone in the fire today, while Charlie was always carrying her internal burdens. When she started arching into me and moaned into my mouth, I knew I needed to draw back. Because I always wanted more with her.

With a last swipe of my tongue, I pulled back slowly, catching her bottom lip with my teeth. I held her close against me, looking into her smoky, sultry gaze.

"I need to go."

"Why?" she murmured.

"Because I can't kiss you and not want more," I said, my lips tugging at the corners with a smile. She appeared to have forgotten she said she needed to talk to Emily.

Her shoulders rose and fell with her breath, her breasts pressing against my chest. She wrinkled her nose and cocked her head to the side. "Okay, okay. Thanks again."

As I reluctantly stepped back, I realized that Waffle was still inside the house. "I need to get Waffle."

Charlie took another step away, turning to open the door. Waffle must've been waiting and dashed out the moment she opened the door.

Late that night, I stood by the windows looking out into the night sky. Stars winked amidst the darkness and the moon bathed the landscape in silver. I wondered if Charlie was asleep yet.

Chapter Nineteen

CHARLIE

The following morning, it was early, and I was already tired. Mom had slept through dinner, but then she'd been up off and on during the night. That was the major downside to when she napped during the day. She never tried to wake me up, but I was a light sleeper anyway. Whenever she was up, I tended to be up as well.

It was now just about 8 AM, and Mom was asleep again. Meanwhile, Em still hadn't gotten up. For the moment, I appreciated the peace and quiet. I made coffee, toasted a bagel, and then sat down at the kitchen table by the windows.

The view here was lovely, but then I'd come to learn the view anywhere in Alaska was lovely. There was a small field behind the house with the forest just beyond it and mountains in the distance. I'd been told the field would be a burst of color once the flowers bloomed this summer. For now, there were a few lingering patches of snow in the shady areas by the trees and frost on the dead grasses from the season before.

The sky was overcast today, suiting my mood perfectly.

I'd tried to talk to Em last night, but I'd gotten absolutely nowhere. Sometimes I wished kids came with an instruction manual. I didn't know what to even be worried about. As a doctor and as a woman who had once been a teenage girl, I also knew it could be as simple as hormones. I mentally reminded myself to call up the local OB/GYN and schedule an appointment for her.

She wouldn't be too thrilled about it. I'd practically had to drag her kicking and screaming to one back in Boston. That was a fight I didn't particularly mind and managed to be practical about it.

As for my attempt to talk to her last night, she was a good enough kid that she hadn't locked me out of her room. Yet, when I'd tried to talk, she'd refused to take her headphones out and simply crossed her arms and stared at me.

Moments like that made me feel as if I was stumbling blindly in the parenting department. I had enough sense to realize that, whether or not a child was biologically mine or not, every developmental stage came with its own set of challenges. Yet, some stages seemed uniquely designed to create a sense of failure for parents. Especially parents who'd been recruited into the job a little too late—such as me.

I'd never even hesitated to consider adopting Emily. I absolutely loved her like she was my own. Yet, I felt as if I'd been playing catch up all along because I hadn't been her mother when she was younger. I'd been her fun aunt all the way up until her mother got sick.

I sat there at the table, sipping my coffee, nibbling at my bagel, wondering how her mood would be this morning and if I could find a way to talk to her. I couldn't shake the niggling worry in the back of my mind about her comment last night.

I'd been so focused on keeping all the balls in the air—between work, my mom, and Emily—that I could see how she might feel like she was lost in the shuffle. Maybe she was the ball that I'd dropped. By the way, I didn't know how to juggle either. I tried once. It was fair to say I didn't have the coordination. At all.

I wondered what Em saw between Jesse and me. Much as I wanted to tumble into whatever was happening between us, her reaction had definitely shown me that maybe now wasn't a good time.

I shoved those thoughts away and took a long swallow of my coffee, watching as a pair of ravens landed in the field behind the house. A magpie chattered loudly from the trees, flying out over them, zooming in like a little plane and then skipping skyward just before it reached them. The rising sun caught the edge of its wings, the blue and green flashing iridescent against the sky for a moment.

I heard Em's footsteps on the stairs and glanced over when she came into the kitchen. Her mood seemed neutral. She certainly didn't give off the irritable, sullen vibe from last night, but she wasn't cheerful either. I supposed I'd have been hoping for too much for that. I stayed quiet until she looked over. "Morning, Aunt Charlie."

Oh good. She was actually speaking.

"Morning. Want a bagel?"

At her nod, I stood and walked over to get one ready for her. As she poured herself some orange juice, I put a bagel in the toaster for her. Within minutes, it was ready. After she sat down at the table, I joined her, wondering how to ask her about her comment last night.

By accident, I managed to be decent about the whole picking my battles thing. It certainly wasn't strategic though. I was so clueless about how to deal with Em sometimes that I occasionally chose to ignore things as long as they weren't major, if only because I didn't know what to do.

Yet, Em's comment about Jesse and feeling like I didn't have time for her didn't seem like something I could ignore.

After she got about halfway through her bagel, I glanced over. "So, I thought maybe we could talk about what you said last night."

Her eyes narrowed, and she ran a hand through her messy hair. She looked so young sometimes to me. It was hard to believe she was fifteen, technically three years away from being an adult. She'd already been through so much, much more than any child should have to go through by her age.

"What comment?" she finally asked.

I took it as a win that she didn't shut me down completely.

"When you said I had more time for Jesse than you. I don't mind that you said it. I just want to understand. I would hate for you to feel like that, and I know I've been busy. I mean, I've been running around like a maniac for years, so busy is nothing new, but I want to make sure you don't feel like I don't have time for you. I need to make more time if that's the case."

She looked down at her plate, breaking off pieces of her bagel and scattering them in a circle. "It's nothing. I was just saying it because I was in a bad mood. Are we good?" she asked.

She looked up this time, and I saw the challenge in her eye. There was no reason for me to insist on more from her, so I didn't even though that kernel of worry was still buried in the back of my mind. "Yes, we're good, but we're not done talking," I replied, forcing myself to not let this slide away.

She sighed and stood to refill her orange juice before returning to the table. "I certainly don't need you to use that as a reason to find more special time with me," she said with a roll of her eyes.

This was a bit of a joke between us. I might have smothered her a little in the early months after her mom died. A friend in Boston had helped me get a better perspective on that, encouraging me to be there for her, but not to insist on time with her.

"Lord knows, I know you don't want that," I countered with a laugh.

She slouched into the chair across from me again and started nibbling on the pieces of her bagel. "Look, we haven't talked much lately, and I know you don't love talking about stuff, but I just want you to know I'm here if you want to talk."

I waited, almost holding my breath to see how she'd react. My words felt too basic, but I didn't know a better way to say what I meant—just that I was there if she wanted to talk.

After a few minutes, she looked up again. "I was in a cranky mood because a guy I liked at school likes this other girl. I was really embarrassed because I thought he liked me."

"Oh, Em. I'm sorry. That sucks," I replied, meaning it completely. Because it sucked. Adolescence was such a fraught time to begin with that the reverberations of social slights were amplified.

"Yeah. It totally does. And he's stupid. The girl he likes is pretty, but she's mean," she said with a sigh.

I sighed along with her. "Things like that happen. I wish I could tell you they didn't, but they do."

"Hey, thanks for the cheer-up advice," she said, rolling her eyes as she laughed.

After a beat, her laughter faded and she cocked her head to the side. "I meant what I said."

Unsure what she was referring to, I arched a brow in question.

"The thing about saying you didn't have time for me. I didn't mean it. I was just feeling bitchy. It doesn't make it okay, but..." Her words trailed off with a shrug, her cheeks turning pink.

I knew it was big for her to be open like this, not just with me, but with anyone. My chest felt tight. Breathing through it, I reached over to squeeze her hand. "Thanks for letting me know, but you need to know if you feel like I don't have time for you, I want you to tell me. Okay?"

Her clear gray gaze held mine before she nodded.

My mom came down the stairs at that moment, effectively ending our conversation.

———

Jesse texted later, asking about stopping by again and how Emily was. I told him tonight wasn't a good night. I didn't know if any night was good. Even though Emily had said she only made her comment out of anger, it worried me. My life was all kinds of complicated. The more time I spent with Jesse, the more I realized my heart was getting in deep. I didn't know if that was such a good idea.

JESSE

Monday rolled around, and I swung by Firehouse Café for coffee and a dose of sanity from Janet. I hadn't seen Charlie since Friday, and it was bugging the hell out of me. Because here was the thing, I fucking missed her.

I couldn't say what I had planned when it came to her because nothing had been planned. I sure as hell hadn't planned on getting tangled so deep into her that I'd miss her over a few days and be bothered by my internal unrest.

Strolling into the café, I glanced around to find Beck waiting in line. Beck was a good friend. He'd been at the station since before me. We'd been on a crew together at one point. With a few changes shuffling things up, we were currently on different crews.

"Hey, man," Beck commented as soon as he saw me.

Pausing beside him in line, I glanced over. "Hey, yourself. How's it going?"

"Well, we have a kid who won't sleep through the night, so I'm fucking tired all the time man. Crazy thing is it's Max. He's just not a good sleeper. Carol's only three months old, and she sleeps like a champ so far," he said, shaking his head slowly. "Gotta tell ya, I love kids, but the lack of sleep is hard."

Even with Beck being this blunt about how tired he was, he was as good-natured as ever. He was definitely an easy-come, easy-go kind a guy. Ever since he'd fallen for Maisie, he'd settled right down too. It was hard to believe that he had once been known as an outrageous flirt who didn't even consider the idea of anything serious. He'd stepped into being a devoted husband and father as if it were a second skin and loved it.

"Good to know. I'll take that under advisement," I offered with a grin.

We stepped forward as the line moved ahead. He glanced back to me. "So, what exactly were you doing taking Dr. Lane and her mother down to the Bird Fest?"

Another thing about Beck was he never hesitated ask any damn question he wanted. Most guys tended to hang back and wait and see if they were curious. *If* being the operative word there. Not Beck. He was nosy as hell.

"Her mom really wanted to go, so I offered to take them," I finally said. As I answered, I realized whatever Charlie and I were, it was vague and entirely between her and me. I didn't want it to be that way. I wanted it to be an actual thing, something concrete.

"So you randomly offer to give people rides now?" he asked with a sly grin.

I chuckled. Beck was no fool. Despite his laid back attitude, he was damn perceptive. "They live right next door to me. And, I might have a thing for Charlie."

Beck chuckled. "Thought so. Told Doc I couldn't see her because she's so pretty. Don't take that the wrong way. I feel nothing for her. It's just weird to see her at the doctor's office. I mean, you know." He nodded vigorously as if I should understand.

I burst out laughing. "I get it, man. Anyway..."

I hesitated because I wasn't sure about asking about things like this. Hell, I'd never had a reason. Beck was a good guy to talk to though. We grabbed our coffees. Glancing over, I asked, "Hey, you want to sit down for a few minutes?"

Beck immediately agreed. He wasn't one to pass up any chance to take a break. After a few sips of my coffee, I looked over at him. "I think I need relationship advice," I said bluntly, cutting straight to the point.

Beck cocked his head to the side, took a long sip of his coffee and then nodded slowly. "I thought so. I saw the way you looked at her. You've seriously got a thing for her. For what it's worth, I don't really know her well. But, I definitely think you're either all in with her or not."

I couldn't help but chuckle. "My question was more along the lines of how to get her to understand I'm serious."

Beck stared at me for a beat and then ran a hand through his hair. "You got to just lay it out on the table, man. That's what I had to do with Maisie. The difference with you and me is she thought I was just a flirt. She didn't take me seriously at all."

"It's that simple?"

"Dude, I'm no expert. But I don't get the feeling she's a casual kind of woman. Honestly, she's kind of uptight. If she doesn't think you're taking it seriously, she'll probably treat you like something to put in her calendar. Seriously, if she matters, tell her."

I wasn't quite sure how to take his advice, although I tended to agree with him on Charlie. I didn't get the sense she expected much from me. Rather, I sensed she was surprised. Seeing as I was too, that wasn't a shock. Yet, she kept the boundaries clear in her life. If she didn't know I was serious, I sensed Beck was spot on. She'd keep me at arms' length and make sure it was clear that it was nothing more than physical.

I might not know what the hell I was doing, but I knew she wasn't just a spin between the sheets for me. With that in mind, I headed into the station. The day was busy. We responded to several calls around town and then got called out to a major fire out in the backcountry.

For the first time ever, I wasn't sure how I felt about leaving town. Normally, I didn't blink when we were called out somewhere. Yet today, I did. If only because I hadn't had an opportunity to see Charlie in days. There was no chance for that now. Even though fire season was still early, as the snow melted and things started to dry up, early spring could be one of the worst times of year because the landscape was dry.

We were headed out to a fire smack in the middle of the Interior that was threatening several Alaska Native villages, as well as a large hunting and fishing lodge. Amidst the hustle and bustle of the crew getting ready to be flown out, I slipped my phone out of my pocket and stepped outside, quickly dialing Charlie's number.

I didn't expect her to answer because it was smack in the middle of her workday. But I didn't want to just text. As expected, I got her voicemail. Her message was no-frills.

This is Charlie. Leave a message, and I'll call you back.

Hey, it's Jesse. Haven't seen you for a few days. I was hoping to stop by tonight, but we're getting called out to a fire. I'll probably be out for at least a week. Maybe less, maybe more. Pausing, I wondered what to say next and then reminded myself I was on voicemail. *Anyway, reception will probably be spotty. I'll text if I can.* I paused wanting to say something else but uncertain if it was okay. Fuck it. *I'll miss you.*

Hanging up, I headed back to the station, wishing I'd been able to talk to her.

Yeah and what? You can't sort all this out inside of three minutes on the phone.

I shook my thoughts away, striding back into the locker room. Ward was rushing around taking care of a few things.

I checked in with Caleb and then heard the sound of the helicopter landing out behind the building.

Within a half hour, our crew was loaded up and Fred Banks, our pilot for the day, was lifting us up into the air. I watched as Willow Brook receded in the distance. Facing forward, Denali, the centerpiece of Alaska, loomed ahead. The majestic mountain was still covered in snow as it would be all summer.

Caleb glanced sideways at me, catching my eyes. "You okay, man?" he asked.

I shrugged. "Oh yeah." I wasn't up for talking about my internal unrest over Charlie, much less right now. It was a minor thing.

Caleb was quiet, his gaze assessing. I didn't doubt that Beck wasn't the only one who happened to have noticed Charlie and me. Willow Brook was a small town, which meant word traveled like brushfire. It wasn't as if we had been public about anything, but we had gone to Firehouse Café, which for all intents and purposes was close to the center of the universe in Willow Brook. Curiosity or not, I sure as hell wasn't up for any conversation about it. Not just now.

Caleb had been through his own turmoil when it came to relationships in the last year. His ex had moved back to town, and they finally found their way back to each other after a bit of a bumpy road. Someone else said something to Caleb, drawing his attention away from me. I leaned my head back against the seat and watched the landscape roll underneath.

Within an hour, the helicopter was landing at the fire camp. We could see the smoke in the distance and the flames flickering against the sky. This area was scattered with dead spruce. The snow had melted, leaving swaths of dead grasses from last summer, just waiting to be burned to ashes by the flames.

Once we were out of the helicopter, we fanned out

around the fire camp. Caleb and I went with Ward to check in with the crew who'd been on the ground since this morning. The wheels in my mind stopped spinning on thoughts of Charlie as I threw myself into work.

Chapter Twenty-One

CHARLIE

Sinking into my chair in my office, I leaned forward to peel off my lab coat. It had been a long day. Just as I was thinking I would have a few minutes to plow through my emails and take care of some online charting, Rachel poked her head around the door.

"It's Mrs. Stan," she announced.

I couldn't recall how she'd come up with that code name to let me know my mother was calling, but it was effective. As soon as she saw the look on my face, Rachel smiled softly. "It's okay, she's just calling. Want me to talk to her and see if I can calm her down?"

"No," I said with a sigh.

Lifting my hand up, I undid the knot in my hair and let it fall loose. The moment I did that, I recalled Jesse's comment about liking my hair down, and my heart gave a funny little tumble.

Rachel was still standing there, her gaze coasting over me. "Are you okay?"

"Yeah, yeah, I'm fine."

I'd had another few nights of very little sleep. Somehow,

my mother had gotten into a cycle where she was mostly sleeping during the day and then prowling around the house at night. Last night, I'd been relieved that I'd installed the door alerts because my phone had buzzed insistently, waking me when she started to go outside in the middle of the night. I shuddered to even think about how far she could wander in the darkness and what could happen to her.

I could tell Rachel doubted my answer when she cocked her head to the side and crossed her arms. I was just appeasing her and could probably use a pep talk. But I needed to call my mom. "I need to call her. We'll talk later, okay? You headed out?"

"Yeah, I'm actually swinging by Wildlands to catch a drink with Holly. Do you wanna go?"

I shook my head slowly. "I can't. Especially if my mom's stressing out about something. It's best if I just go home."

Rachel held my gaze for a moment, and I sensed she wanted to say more. But she didn't. As I lifted my phone from the desk, she started to turn away before spinning back. "We're talking tomorrow. I know you have a few people to call, and I know Janet talked to you about setting your mom up at some of the groups at the seniors place. You need to do something about this, so that you don't have to worry so much. While I'm on the topic, your mom also needs company," Rachel said bluntly.

Emotion tightened my throat. Swallowing through it, I nodded. "I will. I promise."

I was relieved when that answer seemed to satisfy her. I wasn't lying, it was just that I needed to make it happen. After Rachel spun away, I listened for the sound of the door closing behind her and then I called my mother.

She answered right away. "Where are you? I can't find your father."

It had been a few weeks since we'd had this happen. Yet, that didn't make the bite of grief any less sharp. I felt as if I were walking a tightrope between my intellect and emotion as I tried to navigate this process with my mother. Again and again, my emotions threw me off balance. I tried to blink back my tears, but I couldn't. Gripping the phone tightly, I did my damnedest to keep my voice level as I spoke.

"I'm on my way home soon, okay? I'll grab some pizza."

It was a good thing I didn't mind completely abandoning any attempt at cooking. Lately, it felt like take out and quick reheated meals were about the best I could do. I actually liked to cook. I just didn't feel like I had the time.

Blessedly, my mother accepted that answer. I ended the call after confirming with her that Em had come home straight after school. Her grasp on some things was loosey-goosey. Yet, when it came to schedules, she didn't forget the details. Other things like whether or not my dad was actually alive seemed more difficult. Swiping at my tears, I took several shaky breaths. I knew we couldn't turn back time, but it hurt like hell to witness this shift in her. I felt so help-less, my emotions only layering into that sense of help-lessness.

As I picked up the pizza and then drove home, Jesse was burning in my thoughts. I'd heard his message earlier and instantly felt disappointed. Not because he was doing his job. I knew he needed to do what he needed to do. I was disappointed because I instantly felt the sharp pang of missing him. I'd put him off all weekend, and now he'd be gone for potentially weeks. My worry about Em's reaction had been lingering in the back of my mind.

Let's face it, it wasn't like I'd had a man around recently. In fact, I hadn't dated in years. It had been me trying to hold together what was left of our family, and Em certainly hadn't needed to wonder about me bringing a man into our world. I also had to consider that she hadn't exactly had a good role model for a relationship between adults. Her father had almost never been around, and her mother had hardly dated.

How Em might feel about me getting involved with

someone was a loaded question under the best of circum-stances. These definitely weren't the best of circumstances.

Whether she knew Jesse and I had crazy hot sex twice now wasn't really the point. I didn't know what we were doing, and I certainly didn't know if it was smart to keep letting things go in that direction. I definitely had other things I should prioritize, such as Em and my mother and getting a grip on my own emotional state, which was shaky at best these days.

Yet, simply picking up pizza made me think of Jesse. Thinking of pizza had my mind skipping along to his easy presence around my mother. While it wasn't unique to him, I supposed it surprised me because he was such a man's man. He exuded an innate power and relaxed masculinity, so I'd been surprised at his warmth with her.

I knew perfectly well that Rachel and Janet had a point. The best thing for my mother would be for me to get some help. She was alone too much now. I promised myself as I drove home that I would go see Janet in the morning and make arrangements to go with her to the local nursing home where they had groups for seniors.

Somehow, that felt less invasive than trying to set up someone to come in our home to take care of her.

———

I woke early in the morning, after an only partially restless night of sleep. I'd heard my mom get up around one o'clock and had gotten up to check on her. She'd simply gotten a glass of milk and returned to bed.

My phone buzzed on the nightstand, and I rolled over, rubbing the sleep out of my eyes. Sleepily tugging the phone off the nightstand, I propped myself up on an elbow and glanced down at the screen. It was a text from Jesse. My heart gave a funny little skip, and I suddenly felt sad and I didn't know why.

Hey, actually have a little reception here at the fire camp. We'll be heading out at least for a few days. By the way, I meant what I said. I'll miss you.

I sighed, and my heart squeezed. I hadn't purposefully ignored his message yesterday. I'd finally replied late last night. Yet I hadn't had the nerve to tell him I already missed him.

I felt like a coward.

Chapter Twenty-Two

CHARLIE

A few days later, I slipped into a chair at a table in Firehouse Café. Glancing around, I took a deep breath and let it out with a sigh. While there were people here, the early crowd during the weekdays wasn't quite as busy as it would be in another hour or so. Janet came bustling out from behind the counter, carrying my coffee. She slipped into the chair across from me. Flicking her braid off of her shoulder and cocking her head to the side, she slid the coffee over to me.

"So today then?" she asked.

"Yup. I thought I'd stop by here first and then head back up to pick up Em for school. Do you wanna ride with me?" I asked.

Janet nodded. "It'll be fine," she said, reaching over to squeeze my hand.

You'd think I was doing something terrifying when all I was doing was bringing my mom with Janet to her friend's day groups for seniors. I was just so worried about how Mom would react.

Janet hurried off to take care of a few things while I sipped my coffee. Once she was ready to go, we walked out to my car, a little hatchback that was still holding up after our long drive all the way from Boston. When we got to the house, Em came barreling out with her backpack. Em knew the plan for the day and was on board. My mom followed her out at a much slower pace with her cane. She was being good about using her walker around the house, but didn't like maneuvering it outside. She hadn't argued over using a cane, so I took that as a win. She'd already seen Doc for her follow up and was doing *okay* as far as her hip.

Em clambered into the backseat, her eyes widening a bit when she saw Janet, but she didn't miss a beat. "Hey, Janet, how's it going?"

"Pretty good. You ready for school?" Janet asked.

"Ready as I'll ever be," Em replied with a little shrug.

Em leapt back out of the car to help my mom get in. Once my mom was situated in the back, she looked to Janet, her expression confused. After a moment, recognition dawned in her eyes. "Janet, so good to see you! What are you doing here?"

I breathed a silent sigh of relief she didn't seem concerned about Janet's unexpected presence. "We're going to visit a friend of mine after we drop Em off at school," Janet replied.

I thanked the stars Janet had offered to come along because I knew if it were me, my mom would pester me with questions. With Janet, she simply smiled as if it made prefect sense. We dropped Em off at school and headed over to where Janet directed me. Within minutes, we were there. Simply seeing the place helped me feel more comfortable. Though Willow Brook was small, I certainly didn't know the location of everything here, and I'd never seen this place.

Inside my mind, I had turned it into a large, medical looking facility. Instead, we arrived at a medium-sized home, and it seemed as if we were truly visiting a friend. Following Janet's lead, my mom made her way inside with her cane. The hospital in Diamond Creek had been spot on with their assessment. In Doc Johnson's follow up this week, he'd reported her minor fracture was almost fully healed. Her mobility was limited, but she didn't seem to be experiencing too much pain.

She was being a good sport about it most of the time. If only because she discovered she liked having the support of her walker around the house. I'd gotten four of them for the house—one for each bathroom and one for each floor. That way, she didn't have to worry if she forgot one anywhere.

We followed Janet into a side door, which brought us into the kitchen. It was obvious the home had been renovated with the kitchen updated to a more industrial set-up than the average home would have. Through an archway, the living room was an open and airy space with several small seating areas of chairs and two with tables. At the moment, there appeared to be five or six other elderly people here for the day. A woman with short curly gray hair and bright blue eyes glanced over to us from where she was talking with a woman. She had a warm, motherly feel to her.

"Janet, good to see you," she called as she patted the woman on the shoulder and then walked over to us. "So glad you could stop by."

My mother looked slightly suspicious, but after glancing from Janet to the woman whom I presumed to be Norma, she stayed quiet.

Janet looked from my mother to Norma. "Olive, this is Norma." Her eyes bounced to me as she gestured between us. "And this is Charlie."

I didn't know what Janet had said to Norma before, but she seemed entirely on board, chatting casually as if we were friends visiting. I supposed, in a way, we were.

Within minutes, Norma had my mother situated over with a group of women who were having tea. A few of them were doing crossword puzzles, another was knitting, and another few were playing cards. A video game on the television in the corner provided a soft hum in the background.

When my mother glanced that way curiously, Norma smiled. "Howard's grandson gave him that game, so he likes to practice," Norma offered with a chuckle

My mom was delighted with that. Somehow, Norma gradually incorporated my mother into the card game. Once she was busy, Norma walked us to the door. My worry must've shown on my face. "Don't worry. I'll call you if anything comes up," Norma said.

Janet's steely, but understanding gaze met mine and gave me the fortitude I needed. "What time should I plan to pick her up?" I asked.

"She can stay all the way through dinner if you'd like. My schedule rotates. Today happens to be one of my late days, so I'll be here until eight. We have other staff too because we do have some full-time residents."

I absorbed that and felt myself slowly nodding. "Well, if she's having an okay day, why doesn't she stay through dinner?"

"Of course," Norma replied, her cheeks rounding up with her smile.

Stepping back over to the table, I leaned over. "Okay, Mom. I need to get to work. Norma said you can stay if you'd like. How's that sound?"

Blessedly, my mother looked up, almost distracted. "Of course. You go to work. I'm all set here."

Marveling at how smoothly that had gone, I left with Janet. Looking over at her once we got in the car, I took a deep breath and let it out with a heavy sigh. "Thank you. We'll see how it goes, but I needed that."

Janet met my gaze, her brown eyes crinkling at the corners with her smile. "I think it will go just fine." She paused as if considering her words. "You know, I didn't say something to you about this just because I'm nosy. I'll be the first to admit I can be a busybody," she offered with a little laugh. "But I went through something similar with my mother. As I'm sure you can guess with me, I wanted to take care of everything myself. That wasn't smart. Not in the long run. Just like a lot of people, my mother struggled with change and new things. I would imagine once she's adjusted, your mom will enjoy spending time there."

"I think you're right. I guess I just needed, well, maybe more than a nudge. Between you, Rachel, and Holly, the three of you were going to make sure I got some help. I need it, and so does my mom. So thank you again."

Janet gave a wave when I dropped her back off at Firehouse Café a few minutes later. I headed into the office with a sense of relief. I spun into a busy day at work and completely forgot my worries for once.

Jesse danced along the edges of my thoughts, and I wondered how things were going for him. Yet, there was no way to find out, seeing as he was out in the middle of nowhere as far as I knew. I contemplated texting so that if he had a chance to check his phone and was in an area where there was reception, he might get it.

Before I knew it, I'd pulled my phone out and was texting him.

I hope you're OK.

I started at the screen, wondering if I should just tell him what was circling in my mind and heart. The truth was I missed him. Before the thought had come to a conclusion in my mind, I found my thumbs tapping away. It was only three words. The moment I hit send, I wanted to take it back. Because I didn't know if now was the time. But it was too late since I'd already hit send. My cheeks hot, I put my phone down and hurried onto my next appointment, wondering if I was crazy.

Chapter Twenty-Three

CHARLIE

A week later, I sank into a chair across from Rachel at Wildlands. With a few bumps, my mother's transition to spending her days at Norma's place was turning out to be a good choice. It might've been the best decision I'd made ever since my life became one giant mess after another.

Today was one of Norma's late evenings, and Em was spending the night with a friend. That meant I had time to myself that I hadn't had in years. I'd been at my wits' end about what to do with it until Rachel had insisted I come to Wildlands with her.

Rachel glanced over with a grin, her blue eyes bright. "This is so great. You're actually doing something social."

I grinned and rolled my eyes. "You know, it's not like I had anything against doing something social. It's just my life's been a little nuts."

Rachel rolled her eyes in return, glancing up at the waitress who approached our table. I felt my phone vibrate in my pocket just then. Rachel ordered a bottle of wine for us while I slipped my phone out, glancing down to see a text from Jesse.

My pulse lunged, and a smile unfurled from the inside out. I'd had one return text from him since I'd stupidly told him I missed him. I'd tried not to let it bother me, but he hadn't addressed the fact I'd told him I missed him. I felt childish even worrying about it. Hell, he was fighting a fire in the wilderness, he didn't need me being all mopey and weird.

This one made my heart dance. *We're flying home. Should be landing at the station in about a half hour.*

"What's got you smiling?" Rachel asked after our waitress walked off.

For a moment, I considered shrugging it off, but I could use her advice. "Jesse's coming back. Tonight."

Rachel grinned widely, a slight gleam entering her eyes. "And he's texting you about it?"

My cheeks heated, but I ignored it. "Yes, he is."

"So what the hell are you gonna do about it?"

I'd told her earlier this week over lunch at the office about my unexpected—shall we say encounters?—with Jesse and my mixed feelings. She'd point blank told me I should stop letting my life be an excuse.

"I don't know."

"Well, I think you should tell him to meet you here. You have the night to yourself, so you might as well make the best of it."

"I still have to pick my mom up at eight."

Rachel glanced at her watch and then back to me. "That's almost four hours away."

This happened to be one of the days our office closed at 3 PM. We had two early afternoons like this to accommodate for the two late evenings. Before I had a chance to reply, Holly arrived to join us, bringing along her friend Ella. Within the next few minutes, three other women had joined us. Amelia and Lucy, who owned a construction company together, along with Maisie, whom I actually knew.

I'd initially met Maisie when she came into my office

with her husband Beck after a minor hand injury and then had subsequently learned she was the dispatcher at the station. She often called over to our office to give us a heads up when any of the firefighters were headed our way with minor injuries.

I'd all but forgotten what it was like to relax and spend time with friends. Though these women were mostly acquaintances, I could see how they could become friends. Rachel and Holly were the two I felt close enough with to call friends.

Maisie ended up sitting beside me. I was a little tipsy when she glanced over and smiled. "So, I hear you're seeing Jesse."

Huh?

This was so out of the blue that I had no idea how to reply. Amelia was sitting across from me beside Lucy. They were quite the contrast in appearance. Amelia was tall with amber hair and eyes. She nearly towered over Lucy who was tiny and petite with blond hair. She looked quite like a fairy. Except for the fact that personality-wise she was anything but. She was sly, sarcastic, and blunt.

I was surprised when Lucy caught my eyes, a hint of understanding there. "Oh, I forgot. You're kind of new here. It's a little hard. Everybody knows everything. This rumor all got started because you guys were at Firehouse Café and apparently Jesse took you and your mother to Bird Fest. It's been determined, according to the rumor mill, that no man takes a woman and her mother anywhere unless something serious is happening."

With my cheeks flaming, I took a gulp of my wine and looked around the table. I started out by sputtering, "He lives right next door, he just offered to help."

Holly, who was sitting opposite of me from Maisie, elbowed me and shook her head. "Oh no, he was checking you out the first time I saw him at the hospital with you."

I looked to Rachel, almost in desperation because she was my friend. I knew I was blushing, but I didn't know how to navigate this. Muddling my state was the little thrill that coursed through me.

Rachel was no help. She merely shrugged and laughed. "Yup. He couldn't stop staring at your ass."

I took a deep breath and let it out, mentally giving up the fight. "Fine. I don't know what's going on with us."

Five pairs of expectant gazes stared back at me.

"So it's like that?" Amelia asked.

Next from Lucy. "Well, what do you want?"

I fell silent inside and out. Such a simple question and so important. The answer came quickly and a curl of warmth spun around my heart at the thought of Jesse. If I could've wiped away all the complications of my life on a dry erase board, what I wanted was a chance. With Jesse.

When I was with him, it was so easy. Sex, for example. Yet, it wasn't just that. The give and take between us was simply comfortable. It was hard to remember that he'd initially gotten under my skin.

Yet, that wasn't my life. I couldn't wipe it away. Just like those people who ruined things with permanent marker, I couldn't bring back my father, I couldn't bring back my sister, and I needed to take care of Em and my mother. I had absolutely no idea how Jesse fit into the messy equation that was my life.

"Well, my life is kind of complicated," I started. As I said the words, I realized I'd said them so often in the last few years, it was almost a habit.

Holly spoke first. "Everyone's life is complicated."

Rachel nodded, rather emphatically. "Exactly what I've been telling her. If you ask me, it's obvious you like him. So don't let your life get in the way."

Maisie's voice came over my shoulder. "Yeah, Beck says Jesse likes you."

Feeling as if I was rubbernecking as I looked around the table, I spun to Maisie, meeting her gaze. She was quite adorable with her riot of dark curls, her wide brown eyes, and her freckled cheeks. She looked dead serious at the moment.

"I'm sorry, I don't understand," I managed.

Maisie simply repeated herself. "Beck said Jesse likes you."

Amelia laughed from across the table. "Obviously, Charlie wasn't aware that Beck talks to everybody. I swear to God, in some ways he's like a woman."

Maisie laughed. "He totally is. He talked to Jesse about you. Speaking of being like a woman, he came home and told me about it." My eyes widened, but she patted my arm. "Don't worry, he doesn't really gossip. He just tells *me* everything. Sometimes I don't really want to hear it."

I had no idea what to think about Beck's perception, yet the corner of my heart that oh-so-desperately wanted Jesse was waving its arms and bouncing up and down. While I was absorbing this astonishing detail, Ella took a call. She looked over to me as soon as she set her phone down. "Jesse's on the way over with Caleb. They just landed. He said they're showering and then they'll meet us here."

"Jesse knows I'm here?"

At this point, I felt as if I'd entered an alternate universe, one where everyone knew everything. It was so small town, I didn't quite know what to make of it.

"Yeah, I told Caleb. He asked who I was with, and you're here, so..." Her words trailed off with a warm smile. With her glossy brown hair and green eyes, she was lovely. She was the quietest one of the bunch, but she appeared to absorb every detail.

Rachel looked beyond happy about this. "Oh this is perfect. Now you don't have to worry about how much wine you drink. Jesse can take you and your mom home."

This was all happening at light speed. Somehow, on my first actual social event in years, I was surrounded by women who apparently had an opinion on my love life despite its clear uncertainty. I felt as if I had a group of cheerleaders. I just didn't quite know what they should be cheering for.

JESSE

Walking with Caleb through the back hallway of Wildlands, I stepped through the entrance into the bar and restaurant area. My eyes swung around the room like a divining rod looking for water. In this case, the water was Charlie.

The fire had kept me busy. Thanks to the grueling work of getting it under control, I'd managed to wind down the spinning wheels in my mind about her. When we arrived back at the main fire camp and I saw her text that she missed me, I'd nearly let out a whoop. The only thing that had stopped me was the presence of my crew.

My eyes found Charlie. She was sitting at a table with a number of other friends. Her hair was down and my heart squeezed at the sight. I knew it was more than lust when it came to her, but that didn't change how powerful my desire for her was. It flashed to life the moment I was near her.

Caleb and I threaded through the tables to reach the group. He leaned over to drop a kiss on Ella's cheek, only to have her pull him close for more. I'd have given just about anything to kiss Charlie like that, but I sensed now was not the time.

Maisie smiled up at me, shifting over a chair and patting the seat she'd vacated immediately beside Charlie. "Here you go," she said cheerily.

Charlie's cheeks flushed with her smile, and my heart gave a hard kick. Damn, I'd missed her. I slipped into the chair beside her, relieved when conversation immediately picked up around us. A few of the other guys from the station were filtering in to join the table. It was enough of a distraction that no one paid much attention to us.

"Hey," I said softly.

She looked up, her smoky gray gaze darkening. "Hey," she returned. "How are you?"

"I'm glad to be home is how I am. You?"

She cocked her head to the side, as if considering her answer. "I think I'm good."

"I didn't expect to see you out."

With Emily and her mother, I'd expected her to be home. I'd been planning to text and offer to bring pizza. It was a more than pleasant surprise to find her here.

She laughed softly. "I didn't expect to be out either. Em's at Kayla's for the night, and my mom is actually having dinner at Norma's place. I got her set up there last week with Janet's help. Tonight's one of the nights when they have dinner. I still need to pick her up later, but I had a few free hours, so..." Her words trailed off with a shrug, her lips curling at the corners.

I wanted to kiss her.

At this point, Holly leaned around Charlie, catching my eyes. "Right, you're gonna have to be the driver. Charlie's already had two glasses of wine. I was planning to take her home, but you live right next door. You don't mind do you?"

"Not a problem with me," I replied, winking at Holly. She flashed a grin, which led to Charlie throwing a glare her way.

Charlie looked back to me, shrugging sheepishly. "Thanks," she said softly.

A waiter arrived to take our orders, and the evening blurred into casual conversation and dinner. I was starving so the food was downright amazing. Yet, what I savored was the feel of Charlie's presence beside me. Whenever I returned from a stint out in the backcountry dealing with a fire, I was glad to be home, but usually weary. It was damn hard work, and this past week had been no exception. Yet, Charlie's presence took the edge off my weariness.

As the evening wore on, she nudged me with her elbow. "We should go," she said, leaning over so I could hear her voice over the hum of conversation.

Glancing over, my gaze collided with hers. I was so damn tempted to kiss her. I didn't think she'd quite appreciate a public display like that, not just yet.

"Whenever you're ready," I said, not even bothering to resist the urge to slide my hand on her thigh and give it a squeeze. I heard the soft hiss of her breath, satisfaction rolling through me. I loved knowing that maybe, just maybe, she was as powerfully affected by me as I was by her.

A few minutes later, we stepped through the back hallway out into the dusky evening. Swan Lake spread out before us just beyond the parking lot behind Wildlands.

The sun was setting in the distance over the trees and the mountain ridge. The sky was shot through with red and orange as the darkness slowly claimed the light. The lake's surface shimmered with the colors.

Charlie paused beside me, leaning back to look up at the sky. When she glanced to me, I caught her hand in mine. I needed to touch her, craving that point of contact.

When she smiled, it was like the sun coming out after days of rain. I'd managed not to dwell too much on her over the past week. The only thing that had made that possible was the brutal pace of our work. We'd left the area with the fire under control, but only after days of intense work to create firebreaks while the air team did their part to help us out.

There was that fire, and then the one burning between Charlie and me. The banked embers were sparking to life now that we were close again. I was beginning to think there was no way to put this one out. The most I could do was contain it.

With her hand held in mind, we walked to my truck. Opening the passenger door, I held it while she climbed inside. "Charlie..."

She looked up with her foot still resting on the running board. I stepped in between her knees and lifted a hand to slide my fingers through the ends of her hair.

"So you missed me?" I asked.

Her eyes widened and then darkened. I could see the rapid flutter of her pulse in her neck. Her tongue darted out to swipe across her bottom lip. She nearly did me in with that.

"I did," she finally said, her voice husky.

I couldn't wait any longer to kiss her. Sliding my hand into her hair to cup her neck with my thumb brushing along the soft skin, I angled forward and fit my mouth over hers.

It was as if a whip cracked through the air, loud and sharp. That electrifying point of contact set me on fire, heat sizzling through me.

Charlie's hand slid around my waist as she arched toward me, pulling me closer. Her tongue tangled with mine, and she moaned softly into my mouth. For a moment, I lost myself in the scent of her, in the feel of her hot, sweet mouth.

The sound of a door slamming somewhere in the parking lot broke through the haze in my mind. Drawing away reluctantly, I opened my eyes to meet her gaze. "That's a good thing," I murmured. "Because I missed you too."

Charlie didn't say anything. She simply held my gaze, something flickering there that I didn't quite know how to interpret. I sensed it was taking an effort for her to let down her guard. Not with me specifically, but more around the idea of what we might be to each other.

Rounding the truck, I climbed in, a destination in mind. The space in my truck was quiet as I drove. Charlie didn't even ask me where we were going. I was all about being supportive and getting her mother home. But I knew I had another hour before we actually needed to pick her up, and I intended to make good use of that time.

Within a few minutes, I turned down a side road, driving through some trees and then we came out to a clearing where a small lake was visible in the falling darkness. If Charlie had been paying attention, she seemed surprised now. Her eyes swung to mine.

"Where are we?"

I couldn't help but grin. "Just a place where we can have some privacy before we need to go get your mom. I thought about driving home, but this was better."

I didn't say aloud that I'd been worried if I drove toward home, she'd immediately say we needed to pick up her mother first. Nor did I say aloud that I was desperate for her. I had some pride.

She let out a breathy laugh, the sound sending another lash of that whip against the need burning inside of me.

As we stared at each other, the air around us felt heavy like the air before a storm—intense, weighted with the power it was about to unleash.

My truck had a bench seat, handy at the moment. I simply reached across, sliding out from under the steering wheel, and pulled her onto my lap. Charlie got with the program right away. She sighed and settled her hips down over the hard ridge of my cock. Lifting a hand, she smoothed my brow, her fingertips trailing over my cheekbone and down to trace my lips. I caught her finger in my teeth, and a little sound came from the back of her throat. Sweet hell, she just about did me in every damn time.

Then, we were kissing—soft kisses, hard nips, gentle

bites. Just devouring each other. Her hands were everywhere, but then so were mine. I wasn't quite sure how it happened, but she had my shirt torn open and was tugging at the buttons of my fly. I let out a low groan. She shimmied off of my lap, leaning forward and taking me into her mouth. With my hand tangled in her hair, she proceeded to drive me absolutely insane.

Looking down, I noticed she still had her leggings on, so I shoved them down around her hips. Delving between her thighs, I groaned when I found her slick, wet heat. Her hips shifted back into my fingers when I sank them inside of her. I was hanging on by a thread, and I needed to be inside of her. Badly.

When I murmured her name, she rose up. At the sight of her swollen lips, her flushed cheeks, and the wild, tousled mess of her hair, I almost came right then. Her blouse and bra hung open. Her nipples were dusky pink, taut and all but begging for more, so I leaned over to swirl my tongue around one. Catching it lightly in my teeth, I savored the sound of her cry.

Lifting my head on the heels of her gasp, I met her eyes. "I need to be inside of you. Now."

She didn't hesitate, rising up and shimmying her leggings all the way down so she could kick a foot free along with her panties. Straddling me, she never looked away. She reached between us and guided me into her tight, slick channel.

My head fell back against the seat with a low groan as she settled her hips down, wiggling them for good measure.

"Fuck, Charlie. You feel so damn good."

She sighed, the sound squeezing my heart.

Chapter Twenty-Five

CHARLIE

I stared into Jesse's eyes—need reflecting back to me. My heart was thudding so hard and fast against my ribs, I could hardly breathe. With him filling and stretching me, sensation spun inside, little pinwheels of pleasure scattering through me.

I couldn't look away, nor did I want to. The ambient light from the last rays of the sun in the distance angled through the truck windows. It felt as if we were all alone in the world, contained in a bubble shimmering with desire and intimacy.

Jesse's palm slid up my back, sending shivers and lighting little fires under my skin. He swiped his tongue across mine and then his palm slid back down my spine to grip my hips. I couldn't wait anymore, shifting to slide up and down, the feel of him filling me again and again almost making me delirious. If a person could be a drug, Jesse was the one for me.

When we were like this, it was easy, so easy. And it felt so damn good. Intense pleasure banked inside of me with each rock of his hips into mine. Even though we were moving slowly, I felt wild inside, need racing through me so fast, it felt as if I were caught in a riptide. I was needy and greedy, specifically for him. Sensation spun inside, a wave rolling into itself.

When Jesse murmured my name, his fingers digging into my hips as I rose up and sank down again, the wave crested. My climax pulled tight inside and then spun loose, wave after wave crashing through me.

I dimly heard myself crying his name and then felt the heat of his release as he held me tight against him, his hips flexing as his body went taut. With a rough cry, he relaxed.

My head fell against his shoulder, my breath coming in gusts. I rested there as his palm made slow passes up and down my spine. I'd have been quite content to stay there forever, my skin damp against his, with him buried inside of me.

Reality intruded in the form of him murmuring my name.

"Charlie?"

"Mmm, hmm?" I murmured against his shoulder.

"I think your phone is buzzing," he said, his voice gruff. His hand sifted through my hair.

I reluctantly lifted my head, looking at him. God, he was a beautiful man. With his dark amber hair and rich green eyes in the wispy light, the shadows only deepened the strong lines of his features. I let myself scan his face and flick down to the muscle planes of his chest. There was something so sexy about a man who was as fit as he was, not because he worked out, but because of the way he lived.

I completely forgot what he had said.

Until his mouth curled at one corner in a half grin, sending my belly into a lazy little flip. I was too relaxed and satiated for it to be anything but lazy. But even lazy, only Jesse had that effect on me.

"What?"

"Your phone," he reminded me.

"Oh."

I gave my head a little shake. I didn't want to move, so I glanced around for my purse, finding it on the floor on the passenger side. Leaning over, I reached down and deftly caught the strap to pull it up. Slipping my phone out, I tapped the screen and glanced down, suddenly worried.

"Oh, it's just Norma texting. She said mom had dinner, and we can pick her up when we're ready."

Looking over at Jesse, I thought maybe I should say something, but I didn't know what to say. He was quiet, his eyes scanning my face. I sensed he was thinking something, but whatever it was, he kept it to himself.

Over the next few minutes, we untangled ourselves and put our clothes back together. Then, Jesse was driving away from that magical spot, while I was wishing we could stay.

The rest of the evening wasn't quite as romantic. We picked up my mother, who was tickled to see Jesse, and drove home. When we arrived, my heart felt a little heavy. These shimmering stolen moments with Jesse weren't something I could have every day. I needed to remember that.

I helped my mother inside and stole a quick kiss from Jesse outside the door. Later that night, I lay alone in my bed, staring at the stars on my ceiling. I wondered just what to do about Jesse. What I'd wanted tonight was to fall asleep with him. But I didn't feel right about it. I needed to figure out whether the idea of a relationship was even something I should consider right now.

Talk about a downer. After that absolutely glorious encounter in Jesse's truck, my mind was right back to its old habits, worries running laps in my brain.

Chapter Twenty-Six

CHARLIE

One afternoon, my phone rang at work, but I was too busy to check it. The office had been just nuts so far that day. Within a few minutes, Rachel knocked on the door where I was finishing up with a patient.

After I called for Rachel to come in, she poked her head around the door. "Mrs. Stan is on the phone," she said.

Confused, I glanced over at her. My mother had now been going regularly to Norma's. Since she'd been doing that, she hadn't called a single time during my workdays. She seemed to like it. It had relieved an enormous amount of pressure from me.

Rachel arched a brow, as though I could somehow interpret what she meant by that. Finishing up with my patient, I followed Rachel down the hallway, waiting to speak until we stepped into my office.

"What the hell is going on?"

"It's not your mom, but I didn't know what else to say to get you out of there fast."

"What is it?" I asked, worry spinning inside.

"It's the high school principal. They can't find Emily."

It felt as if I was falling, my stomach bottoming out and dread churning inside. I nearly dropped my phone twice trying to call back. Rachel waited with me.

"Yes, this is Charlie Lane, I'm calling about Emily Lane," I said as soon as the receptionist at the high school answered.

"Oh, just a moment," she said.

I bit back a curse. I didn't need to let my impatience get the best of me.

The cheery hold music played while I waited. Finally, Principal Anderson got on the line. "Hello, Dr. Lane, how are you this afternoon?" she asked.

"Where's Emily?" I asked in return, completely skipping past any polite conversation.

"Well, we were hoping you could help us with that," the principal replied. "The last few times she hasn't been in her afternoon classes you've sent a note in with her. But today, there is no note, and she left classes after lunch."

Fear, anxiety, and anger flashed through me all at once. Because obviously I hadn't been turning in notes for Em to miss afternoon classes. But I didn't want to get into that just now. The immediate issue was to figure out where the hell she was.

"Um, okay..." My words trailed off because I had no fucking clue what to say here. Remember how I said I wanted an instruction manual? Said manual would definitely include instructions on what to say to the principal when you found out your niece had been skipping class and forging notes from you.

As I was internally fumbling for what to say, the principal filled the silence for me. "Emily's a good kid. Her grades are excellent. Otherwise, I might've called you and said perhaps she shouldn't miss so many afternoon classes, but she's a straight-A student."

Again, I stood there silently on the phone, looking to Rachel in a panic. Rachel shrugged and stepped over to me, curling her arm around my shoulders and squeezing lightly. As if that would somehow help. I knew she was just doing what she could in the moment, but it was a little funny. I almost laughed at the absurdity of the entire situation.

Uncertain what to say, I finally just said, "Do you mind if I come to the school to talk with you in person? Maybe we can figure this out together."

"Of course not. I'd be happy to talk with you," the principal said politely.

I mean, what else was she going to say?

"Our last bell is ringing shortly, so if you want to wait at least fifteen minutes, you'll miss the rush."

"Okay, I'll be there," I replied.

As soon as I tapped to end the call, I looked over at Rachel. "Em has been skipping afternoon classes and turning in notes that I excused her. Apparently, she forgot to forge today's note," I said with a sigh. I scrubbed my face with my hands. "What the hell do I do?"

"It's probably not an emergency," Rachel said calmly.

"What do you mean?"

"Did you ever skip classes?"

I stared at her and then finally shook my head slowly. "No, actually I didn't."

Rachel arched a brow and shook her head. "Well, I did. All the damn time."

Staring at her, I managed to take a deep breath. I wasn't quite ready to think it was funny, although I was considering the idea.

"Your best bet is to just call her. Right now," Rachel suggested.

I slipped my phone out of my pocket and pulled up her number. Em picked up on the third ring.

"Hey, what's up? The bell's about to ring," she said by way of greeting.

I was so frustrated, I didn't even try for finesse. "Yeah, I know. But you're not there, so I don't see why it matters."

I let that comment just sit there. Em was dead silent.

"Em, where are you?"

She mumbled something.

"Em," I warned. "The principal just called. I know you've been turning in notes, allegedly from me, to excuse yourself from afternoon classes. You forgot today. So, tell me *now* where you are."

Her following sigh was epic. I could practically see the look on her face.

"Fine, I'm with my friend."

"Kayla?" I asked hopefully. Because at least I knew who Kayla was.

Another long, drawn out, and rather dramatic sigh. "No," she mumbled. I'm with Aaron."

Aaron? Who the hell is Aaron?

I was furious and wanted to barrage her with questions about the mysterious Aaron, but now wasn't the time.

"Okay and where are you?" I asked.

"Right here on school grounds. We're out back underneath the bleachers. Before you go getting worried that we're making out, he's just a friend," she offered.

I filed that information away to deal with at another time. "Okay. I'll be at the school in about twenty minutes. I expect to meet you there in the principal's office."

I hung up to the sound of another epic sigh. I didn't even wait to make my next call. I immediately called the principal back and let her know precisely where Emily and Aaron were.

Within another few minutes, I got a return call from the ever friendly principal. She informed me that they'd caught Emily and her friend smoking under the bleachers.

Rachel thought that was absolutely hysterical. While I was furious. Layering onto that, I was even more upset about the forged notes and skipped classes. I wished for the thousandth time that I wasn't doing this alone. I wished I could call my sister and ask her what we should do. But my sister Karen wasn't here for her little girl, the one she had treasured and adored and who was no longer little. No, she was fifteen and skipping classes to smoke with some boy.

I figured Karen probably wouldn't turn over in her grave over the smoking. Although I knew she wouldn't be happy about the lying. No, she'd have been furious right along with me about that.

Looking over at Rachel and letting my phone fall to my desk, I reached up to let my hair down. The moment I did, Jesse danced through my mind. I wondered if I'd ever be able to take my hair down without thinking of him again. Shaking those thoughts away, I focused on the moment at hand.

"Can you let Doc know I had to leave for the afternoon? Also, please have Sandy reschedule the rest of my appointments for today. I need to go talk with the principal and with Em. Even if we finish in time for me to come back, I don't think I should today. I need to take some time with her."

Rachel nodded quickly. "On it." She cocked her head to the side and then tugged me into a quick hug. Stepping back, she squeezed my shoulders. "Hey, this is teenage stuff. It's not the end of the world."

"I know it's not," I finally said, trying to corral the muddle of emotions rushing through me—worry, anger, and disappointment, all colored with the fact I felt like somehow I'd let Em down. "Thanks for the moral support. I gotta go."

———

Later that night, after a pretty bumpy afternoon, I looked across the kitchen table at Em. She was still pissed off at me. She was absolutely furious that I'd called the principal and told her where she and her friend were. Because now she was in trouble not only for skipping class, but also for getting caught smoking on school grounds. You'd have thought I'd practically ruined her life.

My mother had gone to bed, and Em was currently finishing up homework, still stubbornly refusing to speak to me. I didn't particularly care right now. I was rightfully pissed about the smoking, the skipping classes, and the forged notes. After enduring her silence for the afternoon and evening, I decided I was going to talk even if she wasn't going to reply.

"So here's the thing, none of this is okay. Skipping classes is absolutely not okay, smoking is not okay, but lying and forging notes in my name on top of all that is unacceptable. Lying to get away with it makes it all worse," I said flatly, my voice vibrating with fury.

Em sighed elaborately. "Please put your tablet down and look at me," I said.

Without looking at me, she did. "Why do you have to make such a big deal about everything?" she mumbled.

"Because I care about you! This matters. You can't pull stunts like this and think it's okay!"

"It doesn't matter!" she said fiercely. "I just skipped a few classes and smoked a few cigarettes. You're not like my mom! She wouldn't have freaked out like this." At that, she stood, finally looking at me, her eyes dark and her cheeks flushed.

I was so stunned by her words, I couldn't speak. I felt as if she'd punched me right in the heart. She spun around and raced up the stairs, slamming her door shut behind her.

I was frozen in place, the anger I'd felt crashing up against the words she'd just thrown at me. I sat there in the silence, only snapping out of it when I felt a tear roll down my cheek. Standing, I snagged a napkin off the counter and blew my nose. I didn't quite know how my sister would have felt about this. Rationally, I knew it was an easy place for Em to go in her mind—to think I'd handle things differently from her mother. She was likely right, just because we were different. Yet, my sister wasn't here. I was, and we had to find a way forward.

With anxiety tight in my chest, I forced myself to walk upstairs. I couldn't let this slide. I knocked lightly on her door and waited. I barely heard her call for me to come in.

When I opened the door and saw her, my heart cracked. She sat on her bed with her knees tucked up and her arms hugging them tightly. She simply looked sad. She had every reason to be. She had said goodbye to her mother at a young age within months of her grandfather passing. Both of those things had been hard enough on me, and I was an adult. She'd only been thirteen. She'd also had to accept that her father couldn't be bothered to act like a father.

Then, in all my brilliance, I'd decided we should move clear across the country. At the time, I'd been thinking about my mother and Em too because she'd gotten mixed up with the wrong crowd back in Boston. Smoking under the bleachers was nothing compared to what some of those kids had been doing. Yet, none of that changed how hard all of this must've been on Em. Sometimes, I wished I could turn back the clock for myself, so I could have been thinking more clearly in the aftermath of my sister's death.

As difficult as my father's death had been, I supposed we'd all been somewhat prepared for that eventuality. Yet with Karen, I felt as if I'd been slammed by a truck when we found out she had pancreatic cancer. I'd known the grim numbers associated with her diagnosis, and it had terrified me. None of us had been ready, most certainly not Em.

Then, I'd uprooted her from the only home she'd known. I couldn't undo it now, but I wished I could find a way to make things better. Sometimes I worried I relied on her too much with my mom. Yet, they were close, so their connection was also a positive for her. I hoped now that we'd found an option for my mom during the daytime that Em would feel less of a burden.

With all of these thoughts tumbling through my mind, I

held Em's gaze. "I know this sucks, but what happened today isn't okay," I said, steeling myself.

She stared back at me and slowly nodded. "Okay."

I'd been so braced for more push back that I felt as if I'd spun loose on a swing and lost my balance after I got off. "Okay," I managed. "Let's see what the principal decides and then go from there as for consequences. I just want to add that I understand why you might've said what you just said about your Mom. I can't..."

My words trailed off when she sighed again. If there were a world championship competition for sighing, I was fairly certain she would get a gold medal.

She shook her head sharply. "I shouldn't have said that. I don't really know what Mom would've done, but she probably would be mad."

I took a steadying breath. "I know I haven't had enough time for you..."

Another sigh. Pausing, I watched her.

"Oh God," she finally said. "Are we back to that? I don't care about Jesse. I can't believe you think I do."

I took a few steps and sat on the end of her bed. "Okay, well, what's this all about?"

Em threw her hands up in the air, letting them fall to the bed with a thump. "It's just me screwing up! I'm not saying it's okay, but lots of kids skip classes and smoke," she said with a roll of her eyes.

I wasn't about to share with her that Rachel had made that same point. It still didn't make it okay in my mind. Holding her gaze, I shrugged. "And lots of kids deal with consequences. I'd ground you, but you hardly go anywhere. Principal Anderson said something about community service. Let's see what she thinks and if I think you need more consequences at home, we'll discuss it. Okay?"

Em looped her arms around her knees again and nodded, her chin bumping on her knees. Seeing as we seemed to have somehow gotten on level ground, I decided this was enough for now. Standing, I walked to her door. "I expect you to come downstairs for dinner, okay?"

At her nod, I turned and left, closing her door behind me.

The thing was I just didn't know how to juggle all of this. I felt like I was doing everything halfway and, as a result, half-failing at everything.

The other night when I had dinner with Rachel and Holly and met some new possible friends, it had only highlighted how little room I had in my life.

For anything.

Chapter Twenty-Seven

JESSE

Dust kicked up as the helicopter settled down for a landing behind Willow Brook Fire & Rescue. This was shaping up to be a busy fire season in Alaska. Although most seasons were busy for our crews. Alaska was massive, and we also served the Western United States when called. Yet, fire seasons had been getting worse everywhere out West. Climate change had led to drier, hotter summers. With the addition of the swaths of forest ravaged by spruce bark beetle in Alaska, the landscape was ripe to serve as fire fuel.

This time, we'd actually gone out to do some preventative, controlled burns in areas that were considered high risk. Whether fires were planned or not, it was still a ton of work. I was weary, ready for a hot shower, and I missed Charlie.

As I stepped out of a helicopter behind Caleb with Ward following, I watched as Caleb strolled across to the parking lot where Ella was waiting for him. The wind caught her hair as he leaned over and lifted her into his arms. Ward shifted into a jog when Susannah, his wife, came walking out of the station to meet him. She held their baby boy, Wayne, in her arms. When he reached them, he dropped a quick kiss on her lips and then took Wayne. from her, lifting him high in the air and grinning. Ward didn't tend to be the most cheerful guy. Yet, when he was around Susannah, he softened.

In that vein, I wasn't much for standing around watching people. With a shake, I strode past them into the station, heading straight for the showers.

As luck would have it, or in my case not so great luck, I couldn't get a hold of Charlie that afternoon. So after a shower and a stop by Wildlands for an early dinner with a few of the guys from the crew, I headed home. My mother, Frannie, had been checking on Waffle for me while I was away. When I arrived home, she was just returning from walking her.

She glanced up smiling when she saw me. "Jesse! You're home."

"Hey, Mom," I replied, stepping to her and pulling her into a quick hug, while Waffle circled around our feet.

I leaned down and gave Waffle a hug and scratched her neck. "Missed you, girl, how you been?"

Waffle answered with a lick on my chin and a full-body wiggle. Straightening, I walked beside my mother into the house. "I'm assuming everything went okay while I was out," I commented as I tossed my keys on the counter.

My mother leaned against the counter. "Of course it did. Waffle's a sweet dog."

I'd inherited my dark amber hair and green eyes from my mother. Her hair was shot through with gray and quite a bit longer than mine. She had it pulled up in a slapdash ponytail today. She and my father had worked together for years. She helped him run a fishing charter business and did accounting for a few other small businesses in Willow Brook.

I used to wonder how they didn't get on each other's nerves, but then I met Charlie. Being with Charlie was just easy. I supposed I should've thought otherwise, seeing as there was more than just Charlie in that equation. Yet, none of that changed how easy it was to be with her.

My mother cocked her head to the side, her gaze considering. "So, I hear from Janet that you're seeing someone."

I had just opened the refrigerator to pull out a beer and was thankful my mother couldn't see my face. It wasn't that I minded Janet talking with her, it was more that I was a private person. Turning back, I twisted the cap off the bottle, took a swig and then looked over at her.

"Well, I'm not sure what else you need to ask since I'm sure Janet filled you in."

My mother threw her head back with a laugh. Straightening, she grinned at me. "Janet just cares about you. She seems to like this Charlie quite a bit. So tell me about her."

Leaning my elbows on the counter and idly rolling the bottle cap back and forth, I eyed her. "Well, Charlie's my neighbor. She lives right next door with her niece and mother." Pausing, I gestured in that direction. "She's also the new doctor at Doc's office. I'd like to say we're seeing each other, but I don't know if I can call it official yet."

My mother smiled widely. "Oh Jesse, that would be great. I've been waiting for you to meet the right person."

Oh hell. This was news to me. My thoughts must've shown on my face because my mother narrowed her eyes.

"Oh, for crying out loud, get over it. You're thirty-four years old. I would love for you to settle down. I also wouldn't mind some grandkids. I haven't heard a bad word about Charlie around town, so that says something."

I sighed this time, rolling my eyes. "Mom, it's not a huge deal. I don't know why you would take gossip as a barometer of how a person is."

She shrugged, entirely unabashed. "I don't take just any gossip. But Janet's trustworthy. One of the upsides to a small town is if you hear enough rumors that are bad, that might just tell you to at least be wary. But when I can't find anything bad, well, that's a good sign. Janet seems to think she's awesome."

"Well, I'm relieved to know I've got Janet's approval. In the meantime, I'll fill you in when there's more than *maybe* going on between us."

Glancing over, I could practically see the wheels spinning in her mind. "It does sound like she has a lot on her plate. Janet mentioned she adopted her niece and she takes care of her mother."

I knew my mother was simply stating the obvious, but I was instantly defensive. "So what if she does? I don't see why it should matter," I said flatly.

My mother pushed away from the counter, rounding the corner and hugging me quickly. She actually patted my cheek before she stepped away. "Well, that just tells me she means a lot to you. You're my only boy, I think I've been very patient."

I chuckled, realizing she was right about that. I let her other comment go because I wasn't quite ready to get into the details of how I felt about Charlie with my mother. I was still sifting through my emotions myself.

After my mother left, I decided to walk Waffle over to Charlie's place. When I got there, no one was home. I was starting to wonder just where she was. It wasn't that I'd expected her to keep me apprised of her whereabouts, but her schedule was fairly structured with Emily and her mother to work around.

The fact she hadn't texted me back yet, combined with my own uncertainty about pushing the envelope with her had me feeling unsettled. If there was one thing I was coming to understand, it was that I didn't want this thing between us to remain vague and undefined.

When I got back to my place, with Waffle napping on the couch beside me I flipped through a few channels and then texted her again. Even if she was purposefully blowing me off, I didn't like not knowing. She finally replied, only to cryptically say that she was with her mother in Anchorage and they would be there for a few days.

Everything okay with her?

Her reply was quick and too damned vague for my comfort.

Should be fine. Doc recommended some follow up testing due to a fever and a cough she couldn't shake. Things are a little crazy right now. I'll talk to you when I get back.

I might've not have been the doctor here, but if everything was okay, why the hell were they in Anchorage? Willow Brook had a small hospital here. Usually, people only went to Anchorage for more in-depth testing, or actual surgeries.

I knew I shouldn't be frustrated with her, but I was. I was frustrated that she was keeping me at a distance like this, and with myself for us ending up at this point.

Snagging my phone off the coffee table again, I texted Holly. She was a friend after all.

Do you happen to know what's going on with Charlie's mom?

Holly replied quickly.

Yeah. She has an infection, might be pneumonia. Charlie took her to Anchorage for testing and monitoring because we're so small here, we were full. They just went down to the hospital tonight.

The hospital? What the hell? I was suddenly concerned about Olive, far more than I had been after Charlie's general reply that she should be fine.

Mind if I give you a call?

Of course not. Now?

Yep, calling in a sec.

Holly picked up right away. "What's up?"

As soon as she answered, I realized I didn't know what the hell I meant to say to her.

When I was quiet for a beat, she spoke. "Oh, you don't know why you're calling. Let me guess, you're worried about Charlie and you want to do something about it because you're a man and men like to take action. Am I right?"

I laughed. Because she nailed it. "I guess so. I was thinking of heading down to Anchorage. Do you know which hospital they're at?"

Holly sighed. "Oh, Charlie didn't tell you?"

"No, she just said they were in Anchorage for some tests. Look, I'm just gonna lay it out there. I like her. A lot. And now I'm worried about Olive and her and Emily."

Holly was quiet and then she laughed softly. "I told her you had a thing for her, and she didn't believe me. Even I didn't know you'd fallen this hard."

I didn't know what to make of that comment, but I was impatient. "So you were right. Tell me where they are, so I can find them."

"Gotcha. They're at Providence Hospital. Let me know how Olive is when you get there, okay?"

"You got it," I said before quickly tapping my screen to end the call.

I debated whether to leave Waffle here or take her with me and settled on taking her with me. I had a buddy in Anchorage who would let me drop her off. He was one of the guys who'd gotten one of her puppies. I tossed a single change of clothes into a backpack, fed Waffle quickly, grabbed some of her food, and took off.

I called my buddy once I was on the highway. Within the hour, I was pulling up outside of his place. Ben lived in the hillside section of Anchorage just south of town. I had to overshoot the part of town where the hospital was in order to drop off Waffle, but I didn't want to leave her in the car.

Coming to a stop in Ben's driveway, I stepped out, letting Waffle leap past me. "Hey, man," I said as I reached him on the front porch. "Thanks for letting me drop her off for a bit. I might need to crash here tonight if that's okay."

Ben winked, reaching down to stroke a hand over Waffle's back. "Anytime, man. Everything okay?" he asked as he straightened.

Ben was an old friend from Fairbanks. We'd gone to high

school together, and he'd taken a job on the pipeline for a while. He didn't work that job anymore, but he relocated to Anchorage to start a guiding business. He was solid as they came for a friend.

I shrugged. "I think so. I've got a friend whose mom is in the hospital here, so I came down."

Ben cocked his head to the side, running a hand through his short, dark hair. "That doesn't sound like just any old friend."

I chuckled. "It's my girlfriend."

As soon as I said that word, I wondered how Charlie would react. Shaking the thought away, I focused on Ben.

"All right, man. Just give me a call if you're headed back this way later. Don't worry if it's too late. You know me. My place is yours, so just come on in. Actually, you better pop in and say hi to Pancake first."

"Pancake?" I asked with a laugh. "You've got to be fucking kidding me."

Following him inside, I glanced down as Pancake hurried over to us, looking so much like Waffle it was amusing. She had the same lean build and silky black fur with gold markings. She was a tad smaller and full of energy. She spun in circles around us.

Ben met my gaze. "Hey, you're the one who named Waffle. I thought it made sense because she loves pancakes."

"Fair enough," I replied.

"Anyway, now she's met you again. If you show up in the middle of the night, she won't think you're trying to kill me."

After a greeting from Pancake that consisted of licks and wiggles, I left, heading into downtown Anchorage.

When I got to the hospital, I checked at the reception desk, wondering if anybody would even tell me a damn thing. Willow Brook Hospital was a lot smaller. There were any number of nurses who knew me there, but here I was a stranger. Striding to the desk, I paused in front of it. "Hi," I said. "I'm here to check on Olive Lane."

The receptionist smiled up at me. Her blue eyes were kind behind her glasses. When she pressed her finger in the middle of her glasses, pushing them up on her nose, the motion reminded me of Charlie.

She clicked a few keys and then glanced back up. "She's up on the third floor. You'll need to go to the waiting area up there. Take the elevator, go to the right once you get off, and the waiting area is about halfway down the hallway."

The elevator felt way too slow. I wanted to know what was going on. When I stepped off the elevator, I jogged down the hallway, slowing right before I saw the sign for the waiting area. When I turned the corner in the room, I saw Emily sitting in a chair on the far side. Her eyes were red from crying, and her knees were curled up on the chair with her arms wrapped around them. Charlie sat beside her with her hand on Emily's shoulder. Her eyes were also red from crying.

My heart plummeted, dread tightening in my chest. Walking across the room, I glanced around, aware that there were others waiting here. I stopped in front of Emily and Charlie. They hadn't even noticed my approach.

"Hey, is everything okay?" I asked.

Both of them looked up together, their eyes wide. Emily scrubbed her sleeve across her nose. "Hey, Jesse."

"Is Olive okay?" I asked, looking to Charlie.

Charlie shrugged, her gaze controlled. "We're waiting for an update."

"She has a bad fever," Emily said suddenly.

I looked to Charlie as if to confirm. Charlie stood up from her chair, glancing back to Emily. "You okay for a few minutes?"

Emily nodded and rested her chin on her knees. I followed Charlie out to the hallway, wondering just what the hell was going on.

She turned to face me, her features tight. "Now is really not a good time."

Staring down at her, I contemplated what to say. "Hey, I just came to see how you were. If there's anything I can do to help, just say the word."

Charlie looked up at me, pain flashing in her eyes as she twisted her hands. I couldn't say how I knew it, but I knew plain as day that she was about to tell me to leave. I was reacting internally before she even spoke.

"My mom's got a bad fever, and it might be pneumonia. Emily's having a really hard time. I appreciate that you're here, but I just need to deal with this."

"Are you asking me to leave?"

I knew she could hear my frustration in my clipped words. Right about now, I didn't quite give a damn. I was beyond frustrated that she was blowing off the fact I'd made it more than clear what she considered complications weren't that for me.

Yet, it was clear that they were for her.

At my blunt question, her eyes widened slightly. She twisted her hands again and then took a deep breath, squaring her shoulders.

"I guess I am. I don't know how to do this right now. It's just too much."

"Having someone that matters in your life is too much?"

The minute my question came out, I knew it wasn't a great tactic. Not that I could consider anything I said strategic. Not now. At the moment, I was just all reaction. My pain at her pushing me away was spinning into my frustration at the situation. Nothing about my reaction was helpful, but then I didn't have a handle on it.

Charlie's eyes flashed with anger. "Jesse, it's been great. I just don't know if now is the right time for me to be doing... whatever we're doing." She waved towards the waiting area behind us. "I need to be able to be here for Em and my mom."

Staring at her, I tried to marshal my thoughts. But I was hurt, and now I was pissed at how easily she was dismissing me, dismissing us. "Good to know that I was nothing more than a good lay for you."

At that, I spun away, striding quickly down the hallway. I heard Charlie's footsteps behind me, and she caught the edge of my sleeve.

"Jesse, it's not..."

Her words trailed off when I spun back. "I get it. It's not like either one of us made any promises. I suppose I thought you'd notice I was trying to be there for you, rather than seeing me as yet another complication in your life."

Her breath drew in sharply, two bright red spots appearing on her cheeks. She was quiet, simply looking at me.

At that moment, a nurse approached from behind us. "There you are," the nurse called out.

Charlie held my gaze for another beat before turning away. "I have to go."

That was it. I watched her retreating back, stuffing my hands in my pockets.

I ended up not even staying at Ben's place. When I got there, he was in the middle of a call. When he gestured for me to come on in, I shook my head, mouthed *thank you*, and then left with Waffle bounding at my side.

I was too cranky to be good company. I drove home in the falling darkness, watching the landscape roll by. A flock of geese flew above, their calls clear in the quiet night. As I rounded the curve, I saw the silhouette of the flock against the setting sun—bird shadows against the backdrop of orange and red shot through with gold.

Chapter Twenty-Eight

CHARLIE

The sleek fabric of the waiting room chairs was warm against my cheek. Coming awake slowly, I became aware my neck was bent awkwardly toward the wall. The hospital here got points for trying to make a comfortable waiting room. At least the chairs had padding. Yet, sleeping upright under duress was never a great night's sleep.

I had a pounding headache. Glancing around, I saw Em two seats away from me, sound asleep with her knees curled up to her chin. Her short hair stuck up in little spikes. Looking at her, my heart clenched. She looked so young when she was asleep, the lines of her face softened. Her hand was curled around the edge of her jacket, the purple fleece matching her hair.

Straightening, I gave my head a shake. Gathering my backpack, I walked into the restroom off the side of the waiting area. After quickly splashing cold water on my face, I washed my hands and brushed my teeth. Smoothing a brush through my hair, I tucked it into a ponytail. After downing two ibuprofen, I headed out to face the day. First order of business, coffee. Well, after I figured out how my mother was doing.

The nurse last night had assured me they would come check in with me at any point if there were any updates. Nevertheless, I checked in at the nursing station. There was an entirely new crew this morning.

A woman with blond curly hair, a round face, and twinkling brown eyes smiled at me as I approached the desk. "Good morning," she said cheerfully. "How can I help you?"

I gathered she had already had coffee, or at least a decent night's sleep. I managed a wan smile and rested my elbows on the desk. "I'm just wondering if there's an update on Olive Lane. She's my mother."

My eyes flicked down to her nametag—Rosie. Rosie suited her perfectly. She clicked through a few screens and then looked up with another smile. "No updates, but she slept through the night. They'll be doing rounds shortly. You're welcome to pop in and see her if you'd like. Visiting hours start in an hour."

"Do you know when I'll be able to speak with the doctor?" I asked.

I was cognizant of the fact that it was annoying as hell for a doctor to show up at the hospital about a family medical issue and insert themselves into treatment decisions. Yet, it took an active effort not to get pushy and start asking very specific questions. I told myself I would save them for the doctor.

Rosie clicked a few more keys and then looked back up at me. "She should be available in just a few minutes. She'll have a chance to check your mother's chart. Would you like me to buzz her and see if she can come down?"

"That would be great, thanks."

I returned to the waiting room after Rosie assured me the doctor would come find me. Em was still sound asleep, so I slipped into the chair nearby and waited. My mind immediately went to Jesse. While my thoughts were heavily occupied by my mother, there wasn't a lot I could do about what was going on with her right now. Last night, my thoughts had run laps around what to do about Jesse.

I felt awful about how I'd handled things. It was obvious he was hurt and angry. Meanwhile, I was trying to tell myself that last night hadn't been good for him to be around me, but it didn't feel good. In fact, it felt like hell.

I missed him, and even though my life was a mess, I wouldn't mind having a shoulder to lean on. Yet, that made me feel selfish. As if that was the only reason I wanted him around. To have someone to lean on. It was so much more than that.

This other voice—up to now, a voice I hadn't even known existed inside of me – had all kinds of things to say.

What the hell are you thinking? The man obviously likes you. Like maybe even a lot. And you're shoving him away? Why? Because you can't face the fact that it might be worth it to let your guard down.

And so on and so forth. I had to beat back the urge to call Jesse. He wasn't here right now, and I certainly didn't feel like now was a good time to call him. Nor did I know what I would say if I did. I needed to talk to the doctor, check on my mother, and get some damn coffee.

Within a few minutes, Dr. Clark poked her head around the corner in the waiting area and gave me a little wave. She started to walk across the room, but then her eyes landed on Em who was still sound asleep. I stood, gesturing to the hallway.

I'd met Dr. Clark yesterday afternoon, and I liked her. She was no-nonsense with her short dark hair, brown eyes and narrow square glasses. She was sharp and on top of it. She glanced down at the computer tablet in her hand and then back to me. "So here are her vitals for this morning."

She reeled them off and then waited. I laughed when I realized she was giving me a chance to come to my own conclusions.

"Well, it's good to hear her fever's gone down," I said. "It sounds like she's stabilizing. Any ideas what set this off?"

Dr. Clark ran down a few options and then shrugged. "In the end, your mom isn't young anymore. I think she was on the edge of pneumonia, but because of you, we caught it before it got to that stage. It likely started as a simple cold. From what I understand, it's been a rough few years for your family. Her emotional state will affect her health as I'm sure you know."

I leaned against the wall, nodding slowly. "I know. She misses my dad. A lot. She seems happy that we're here but..." I lifted my hands in surrender, letting them fall loosely.

Dr. Clark nodded, understanding contained in her gaze. "Of course. Well, I think with another day or two here, her fever will be gone. By then, I'll feel comfortable for her to be discharged. I would recommend you continue taking her to the day groups. She mentioned that it's nice to have people around. There aren't too many medications that help with dementia, as you well know. But there are a few things we can do to help her when she gets anxious, so I'm thinking that's what we should target. I spoke with Dr. Johnson earlier, and he's in agreement with what I recommended."

She quickly reviewed her recommendations for an as needed medication when my mother got anxious and then gave my shoulder a squeeze. "Your mom is going to be okay. It's an adjustment for the whole family when people start aging. On a good note, her hip is stable. I think she's going to need to keep using her walker. If you can convince her to use the walker outside of the house, that would be great. The cane should just be a back up for now."

"Oh, you'll get no argument from me on that," I offered with a chuckle. "If you could talk to her about it, that would be great."

Dr. Clark laughed softly. "Of course. I'm happy to talk with her. Anyway, she's sound asleep right now. You're welcome to check in on her if you'd like. Visiting hours officially start in about an hour."

"If she's sleeping, we'll let her rest. Any suggestions for a good place for coffee and breakfast nearby?"

Within a few minutes, I returned to the waiting area with the name of a nearby diner. Dr. Clark assured me they served excellent coffee and great omelets. Emily was stretching in her chair as I entered the waiting room.

She rubbed her eyes with her fists and then looked up, smiling sheepishly. "Morning."

"Good morning. Do you want to wash up in the bathroom?"

At Em's nod, she stood and swung her backpack over her shoulder. She had a toothbrush and a change of clothes in there. She shuffled into the bathroom while I gathered my things.

Jesse was still burning in my thoughts, but I told myself I'd have to figure out what to do about him later. Em and I left the hospital to have breakfast and coffee, and I felt halfway human by the end of it.

As I was savoring my coffee and she was finishing up her omelet, she glanced across the table, catching my eyes. "So how come Jesse didn't stay last night?"

I bit back a sigh. She hadn't actually asked about him last night, and I hadn't been up for talking about him, so I'd been relieved. I looked over at her into her wide gray eyes that were so similar to my sister's. Despite Em's attempt to distinguish herself with her spiky purple hair, she was still so much like my sister, I experienced a sting of grief.

Taking a swallow of my coffee, I contemplated my words. She was still looking at me expectantly, and it was clear she wasn't going let *no comment* slide. On the heels of a deep breath, I said, "It wasn't a good time for him to be here last night."

She took a bite of her omelet, chewing it quickly and

then cocked her head to the side after a sip of water. "What do you mean it wasn't a good time?"

"Um, Gram's in the hospital, and you were a little upset last night. I just didn't think we should throw someone else into the mix," I finally said, stumbling over my words a bit.

Em set her fork down and leaned her elbows on the table. "That's just stupid. You always have to do everything alone, don't you?"

She took another bite of her omelet and then sighed. "And you get on my case about having a hard time making friends," she muttered with a roll of her eyes.

I was about to say that Jesse wasn't a friend. But then Em startled me. "Plus, I know he's more than a friend."

I choked on my coffee and had to snag a napkin to wipe some off of my chin. She smiled and, with a flourish, took another bite of her omelet. "Just saying," she said with a knowing grin.

After breakfast, we returned to the hospital. My mom was awake, and we got to check in with her. As the next two days passed, Em and I mostly camped out at the hospital and did a few things here and there around Anchorage. Jesse was always dancing along the edges of my thoughts.

Chapter Twenty-Nine

JESSE

Several days had passed since I left the hospital. I hadn't heard a thing from Charlie, nor had I made any effort to reach out to her. I was starting to feel like I might be being as stubborn as she was, and it didn't quite sit well with me. After a few minutes of fetch with Waffle in the morning, I stopped by Firehouse Café on the way into the station. As I was standing in line, I heard Beck say my name as he approached from behind.

"Hey, Jesse," he said, stepping up beside me in line.

Glancing to him, I managed something like a smile. "Hey, man, how's it going?"

"Well, it'll be better after I get some coffee. I'm working on setting a record for shitty nights of sleep."

"Oh?"

I couldn't help but smile. Leave it to Beck to make it funny that he was tired all the damned time.

"Yeah, man. I told Maisie we should have a contest. My current record is a full two hours of sleep in a row. She got three hours one night."

"So, I'm guessing you're not the kind a guy who leaves it up to her to get up when the baby wakes up?"

Beck shook his head vigorously. "Hell no, man. That wouldn't be fair. Maisie had to be pregnant and have the baby. The least I can do is wake up when she wakes up. I'm not a walking food machine like she is. I usually get up first to check to see what she needs because she's not always hungry. At first, we thought we had the sleep thing made with Carol, but now she's traded places with Max."

I clapped him on the shoulder. "Good man."

We reached the front of the line and Janet's beaming smile greeted us. "Hey, boys. The regular for both of you?"

Beck nodded firmly. "Absolutely. Add an extra shot in mine. I need it."

"Ditto," I replied when Janet glanced my way.

Janet spun away once we paid, greeting someone else and taking their order before prepping our coffees. Beck and I stepped out of line to wait to the side of the counter.

"So how's Charlie?" Beck asked.

That was about the only question I didn't want to answer. I sure as hell didn't know the answer. Before I even said anything, Beck cocked his head to the side. "You don't even know do you?"

"Why do you say that?" I countered.

"Oh, just the look on your face—the 'oh-fuck-I don't-know-what-to-say' look. I know it well. I get it sometimes."

"So what happened?" he asked as Janet stepped over and handed us our coffees. We snagged a table in the corner.

I took several sips of my coffee before I replied to his question. "Well, I think I might've blown it."

"How did you blow it?"

"Well, her mom had to go to the hospital in Anchorage. I went down and she pretty much told me to leave."

Beck cut in. "How is that your fault?"

"I don't really know how she feels. But the way I fucked up was I got pissed about it."

Beck pursed his lips, took a sip of coffee and nodded slowly. "Oh," he finally said.

"That's it? Oh?"

He took a long gulp of his coffee and nodded firmly. "Yeah. I don't know how she feels either because I don't know her that well. But probably not your best move to get pissed when her mom's in the hospital."

"Any advice?"

"Sure. Same advice I gave you before."

"Refresh my memory."

"I told you to lay it on the table. I mean, let's face it, her life *is* complicated. She's taking care of her niece and her mother. She's got some shit going on. So her saying things are complicated, well that's not a bunch of bullshit. But if you can deal with all that and you want to deal with it, then you need to make sure she knows."

I took a deep breath and let it out in a sigh as I nodded.

"This time, you should follow my advice," he added.

I chuckled and took another long sip of my coffee. "I'll try."

Beck ended up having to leave when Maisie called about something he left at the house. I wasn't quite up for heading into the station yet and I still had a little time, so I stayed behind. When Janet swung by to see if I needed anything, I ordered a ham pinwheel and asked her to heat it up for me.

As I was waiting for her to return, the bell over the door jingled. Glancing over reflexively, I saw Charlie walking in. The moment I saw her, my heart gave a hard thump, like a fist to my chest. It was as if my heart recognized her as its owner. I might not have been able to put words to my feelings before, but I knew I couldn't sit back and let my chance with her slide by. I needed to make my feelings clear to her, precisely as Beck had just pointedly told me.

She was dressed for work in slacks and a fitted blouse. I knew when she got to the office, she'd be putting on her giant white lab coat that would hide her delectable body. A smile tugged at the corners of my mouth. She was so buttoned up when she had on her work attitude.

I watched as she walked toward the counter, standing in the back of the line. Her hair was twisted up in a knot, and she was wearing her purple glasses. As I watched, she adjusted them on her nose, reminding me fiercely of the first time I kissed her.

She glanced around, her eyes finally landing on me, widening slightly with a flare of recognition. I desperately wanted to get up and go talk to her, but I was well aware we were in a very public location. Janet might be busy, but I knew she was watching like a hawk.

I forced myself to look away and take another swallow of my coffee. Staring out the window, I watched as people walked along the street. The days were getting longer and the air warmer, which meant more people. I idly wondered if you could do a calculation based on the rise in temperature and the number of tourists that poured into Alaska with every five-degree increase in temperature.

"Janet asked me to bring this over," Charlie said from over my shoulder.

I turned to find her holding a small plate with my ham pinwheel on it. She set it down on the table beside my coffee cup. She clutched her own cup of coffee in her hand, her thumb fiddling with the plastic lid. She stood there quietly, and I wondered if she was going to say anything else.

"How's your mom?" I finally asked when she didn't say anything else.

She nodded quickly. "Okay, she's okay."

"And Emily?"

"Well, except for the fact that she has to do community service because she got caught smoking at the high school, she's fine."

My words came out before I thought it through. "She can do her community at the station if she wants."

Charlie's gorgeous gray eyes widened and a slight smile

curled her lips. "I didn't even think about that. But then I've never really had to think about what kids do for community service when they get caught smoking in school," she said with a little laugh.

"That's probably not on everybody's radar. Just bring her by the station. Maisie'll set her up and call the school to send over the paperwork. She does that all the time for kids who need to do community service."

Charlie nodded and swallowed. She was just close enough for me to see the pulse racing in her throat.

Her next words stumbled out so fast, it was hard to keep up. "I'm sorry I got upset with you at the hospital. I was overwhelmed and stressed and worried. I know you were just trying to help."

I absorbed her words and nodded. "Yeah. I was. Just trying to be there."

She stood there, the sound of her thumb flipping the edge of the plastic lid making a soft clicking sound. "Um, I should go to work."

"Okay, maybe I'll catch you later."

She hesitated for a flash, and I sensed she wanted to say more. Just then, Janet came hurrying over. She held a tray of dishes she'd collected from nearby tables.

"Anything else?" Janet asked quickly, her curious gaze bouncing between us.

"No," Charlie said quickly. "I have to go."

She hurried away. My heart literally ached to watch her leave. With this audience though, I wasn't inclined to follow. Not right now.

Chapter Thirty

CHARLIE

Later that evening, I sank into my desk chair and reached up to unwind my hair. As my hair fell loose around my shoulders, Jesse danced through my mind. He'd pretty much taken up a full-time parking space in there. Running into him this morning had been painful. I had so desperately wanted to say more than I did. Yet, I felt like I was still stumbling along, just barely juggling all the balls I needed to keep my life running.

Coward, that rather assertive voice whispered in the back of my mind.

Tossing the elastic for my hair on my desk, I stood and walked to the windows to look outside. This was one of my late nights, so it was going on seven o'clock. The sun was just now starting to slide down the horizon. The mountains were silhouetted against sky, the stark lines of the ridges and peaks dark against the setting sun. Its rays left streaks of violet and orange in its wake.

The longer I was here in Alaska, the more I understood why my parents had missed Alaska so much. Its beauty was stunning and spectacular. You could feel the heartbeat of life here and realized how small you were in the big scheme of things with the mountains rising tall and the wilderness beckoning.

My chest felt tight and emotion knotted in my throat. I missed Jesse, and I needed to scrabble up the courage to talk to him.

There was a quick knock at my door and then Rachel stepped through. Turning, I leaned my hips against the windowsill, curling my hands over its edge.

"You know, I always know it's you," I offered as she closed the door behind her.

She flashed a grin. "How come?"

"Because you're the only one who knocks and then just comes in. Not that I mind. I kind of like it actually."

Rachel walked over to the windows and leaned against the sill beside me, mirroring my position.

"So, I got coffee at Firehouse Café at lunch today," she offered.

"Okay. That's a little random," I replied, thinking there was certainly nothing unusual about that. Glancing sideways, I saw a gleam in her eyes. "What?"

"Oh, just that Janet said she saw you talking to Jesse there this morning. She said it looked like you'd broken his heart when you left."

I wanted to cry, my chest and throat knotting with emotion. I didn't know if I'd broken his heart, but I felt like I'd broken mine. It was certainly cracked. The crack hurt. Like when you crack the skin on a knuckle, and it keeps tearing open again every time you move your hand. The pain festered and lingered, stabbing at me over and over again as the days wore on.

The gleam in her eyes faded, shifting to worry. "Hey, I was just teasing. Are you okay?"

Suddenly needing to sit down, I stepped away from the windows and sank into the chair across from my desk, curling my knees up against my chest. For a moment I felt like Em. Then, I realized I was like her, or rather she was like me. Tucking my knees up like this was something I'd always done when I was growing up. My sister Karen never had. She used to tease me about being like those roly-poly bugs that curled up in a ball when you found them.

Somehow, I just loved realizing that Em might have inherited this small habit from me.

Rachel sat down in the chair at an angle from me. "Okay, spill it. You've been off for days, but I was chalking it up to everything with your mom. What's going on?"

I proceeded to pour the whole story out—how I'd basically chased Jesse away from the hospital, how he'd gotten angry, and now I didn't know what to do.

Rachel was quiet when I finished and then she sighed, rather elaborately. Looking over at her, I couldn't help but roll my eyes. "You sound like Em. I swear, she could set a world record for her sighs."

"Hey, at least I'm not behaving like a dramatic teenager. *I have to do this all myself!*" she exclaimed, putting her hand against her chest as if overwrought.

"Is that what I sound like?" I asked, aghast.

Rachel's gaze sobered. "Not entirely. I just think you do have a lot on your plate, and you're letting it be a barrier. Jesse's made it more than clear he doesn't have a problem with what you keep calling *complications.* Stop pushing him away. It's obvious you don't want to. In the big scheme of things, everybody's life is complicated. All it would take is a few shifts, and my life could be just as messy as yours. A lot of shit went down in a short period of time for you, but it is what it is. Life is a mess sometimes. Honestly, you can count yourself lucky for meeting Jesse in the middle of all this."

"How do you figure that?"

"Because sometimes we don't know how strong someone can be until shit goes down. He's walking into your life with his eyes wide open. I've seen couples seem hunky-dory, and then shit hits the fan and they fall apart. That's not what's happening here. If you ask me, you need to go talk to him tonight. In fact, before you come up with an excuse that you need to go check on Emily and your mother, I'm bringing them pizza for dinner. We'll have a card night. I'm all over that shit. And they love pizza, right?"

Rachel had joined us for dinners a few times, so she knew my mom and Em liked to play cards together. I started laughing and crying all over again. "Okay, let me call Em right now. I'll tell her you're on your way."

"Oh no," Rachel said as I slipped my phone out of my pocket. She actually snatched it right out of my hands. "I don't think so. Because if she says anything that leads you to think you need to go home, you'll back out of talking to Jesse."

"Hey, give me that," I protested, trying to take my phone back.

Rachel held it high above her head, laughing as I glared at her. "Password please," she called out.

Giving up, I answered, "One, two, three, four."

Rachel looked at me like I was crazy.

"I can't remember anything else. It's not like I have anything to hide either."

"Oh my God, you haven't even been sexting with him. You need to get a life."

———

By the time I turned down Jessie's driveway, my pulse was running along at a high idle. My palms were sweating, and my belly was spinning in flips.

I was so damned anxious.

The one time I'd been over to his house, I had walked through the darkness to get here. It was different to pull up in the front. He had a circular driveway, and I was both relieved and terrified when I saw his truck parked in front.

You can do this, Charlie. All you have to do is tell him you fucked up and tell him... Tell him what? You love him. It doesn't matter if the timing isn't good.

Emotion welled in my throat. Taking several deep breaths as I rolled to a stop, I put my car in park and cut the engine. After a moment, quiet filtered around me. The moment felt weighty, if only because of my own internal state. Stepping out, I heard the sound of Waffle barking. I couldn't help but smile. If I didn't know her, I would think she was tough.

I took another deep breath and hoped I wasn't at the point of hyperventilation by the time I got to the door. I absorbed his house from the front. It looked a little different, but then I'd only seen the back in the darkness. My cheeks got hot just thinking about that night.

From the front, the home blended into the landscape, nestled amongst the trees with dark wooden siding. There was a curved deck on the front with wildflowers dotting the front lawn. On the heels of another deep breath, I followed the flagstones up to the door. I knocked and waited, my heart in my throat beating so loud I could hear it over Waffle's barks.

I kept waiting and started to wonder if Jesse was even home. When he didn't answer, I didn't know what to do with myself. Somehow I was drawn to simply walk home. I wasn't even thinking about it. I forgot that I'd actually driven over here.

Rounding the house, the opening in the trees was visible. The path looked different in the dusk without the moon gilding the trees in silver. Everything felt earthy, the leaves still somewhat damp from the recent snowmelt. A few branches crunched under my feet as I walked. Birds called, and a pair of squirrels dashed about in front of me on the ground, chattering loudly at my presence.

I stopped to take a deep breath, trying to calm myself. The air was crisp and scented with spruce. Everything felt alive, as if the air contained a burgeoning sense of growth, a quickening.

I heard footsteps behind me. Spinning back, I saw Jesse. My heart flew into my throat and tears pressed hot in my eyes. I was an emotional mess.

"Hey," he called.

My eyes absorbed him. He wore faded jeans, the fabric hugging his muscled legs, and battered leather boots. His navy T-shirt didn't do a damn thing to hide the hard planes of his chest. My eyes lingered on the flex of his bicep as he lifted a hand to run it through his dark amber hair.

The setting sun fell through the trees, dappling the ground and glinting off of his hair. The sounds around us— the birds calling, the squirrels chattering—faded as he stopped in front of me.

"I heard you knocking, but I was in the middle of switching laundry over, and I didn't get to the door in time."

"Oh."

Wonderful. I was back to single word sentences with him. I had so many things I wanted to say. They were jostling around in my heart as emotion rushed hard and fast through me.

Jesse simply looked at me. After a beat, his shoulders rose and fell with a deep breath. "Look, I shouldn't have gotten upset the other night at the hospital. I just needed to say that." His voice was low and somber, his eyes pained.

I shook my head quickly. "You don't need to apologize. I do."

"I...I..." The words caught in my throat again, and I kicked through the dam inside. "It's hard for me to say this. I don't like needing anybody. I don't need you because you help and you're nice and you put up with my fucked up life. I need you because I love you and everything comes so easy with you. I don't know quite what to do about it and my life is a mess and I don't want to put it on you. I don't want to make things worse for us and I don't want you to wish that you were crazy later on…"

Most of that came out in a run-on sentence with a few pauses. My words trailed off as I paused to gulp in a lungful of air.

Jesse's gaze softened, the careful, guarded look fading from his eyes. There were only a few feet between us. He closed the distance in one stride, stopping inches away and catching my hands in his. Mine had been flailing about rather ridiculously while I was talking, so that was a good thing. I needed something to hold onto.

"You don't need to apologize either. I think I fell in love with you practically off the bat. I just didn't know it. Because, you see, I wasn't looking for love. I just thought you were hot as hell." His mouth curled at the corner with that, and my belly spun in a delicious little flip, a shuddery feeling running through me. Meanwhile, my heart squeezed and then spun around, practically doing a victory dance inside my chest.

Jesse continued, his green gaze holding mine. "What you just said then, that's what it is for me. It's easy when I'm with you. When I don't worry about the rest, it's just easy. You keep saying your life is complicated, and I'm not gonna argue with you about that. But none of that matters to me. I know you've got stuff going on with Em and your mom, but it's stuff we can deal with. I hate seeing you try to carry it all alone."

I didn't realize I was crying until he dropped one of my hands and swiped a tear with his thumb. Then, he was kissing me, and I burrowed against him, melding my body to his. While I felt wild and crazy inside, as if I were spinning out of control, we were in it together.

I forgot where we were until I heard Waffle bounding through the leaves and felt her soft body wiggling against my legs as she circled us.

Jesse drew back just far enough to speak, his lips moving against mine as he did. "We're in the middle of the woods."

I laughed softly, emotion pressing against my skin. "I know. Can we go back to your place?" I asked, well aware of the feel of his arousal hard and hot against my low belly, and need curling through me in a hot wave.

"You don't need to be home soon?"

"Actually, Rachel's there. We had a heart to heart today, and she told me I was stupid. She took my phone and went to pick up mom," I said with a laugh, feeling my cheeks heat as I answered.

Jesse threw his head back with a laugh and turned, keeping my hand held fast in his. " I suppose I'll have to thank her later."

"Oh, and she says I'm missing out because we haven't been sexting."

Jesse got a wicked gleam in his eyes, and we were practically running the short distance back to his house.

We dashed through the sliding glass door on his back deck. Waffle was still out in the yard, sniffing along the edge of the tress. I paused, looking up at him. "Do we need to call her?"

"Oh God no. She'll be happy for hours," he murmured and then he was yanking on my clothes.

Chapter Thirty-One

JESSE

Charlie stood before me. Her blouse had fallen open, or rather I'd nearly shredded it. Her nipples were damp and pink, taut from my attentions. She sat before me on the kitchen counter with nothing on other than a scrap of black silk that passed for panties and her blouse hanging loosely from her shoulders. Her breath rose and fell in quick little pants. She'd torn my fly open. My cock throbbed as she curled her palm around it and shoved my briefs down around my hips.

I let out a low groan as she swiped her thumb across the top, catching a drop of pre-cum. Looking up at me, she lifted her hand and drew her thumb into her mouth. My knees nearly gave out when she swirled her tongue around the end of her thumb, her eyes locked with mine, silver flashing in the stormy gray depths. Her dark hair fell in a messy tousle around her shoulders. I'd made quick work of the tidy knot she usually wore and set her glasses on the counter. Not that I didn't fucking love how sexy she was in them, but I didn't want to break them.

Dipping my head, I nipped along her neck, needing to

taste her skin. On the heels of her ragged sigh, I lifted my head. "I need you," I murmured.

Hooking my finger over the edge of her panties, I yanked them down over her hips. She helpfully lifted up for me to slide them over her legs and then kicked the black silk panties off her ankles where they fell to the floor in a soft whoosh.

Sliding her hips to the edge of the counter, I gripped my cock, dragging it back and forth through her slick folds. Never once looking away from her face, I lifted my free hand. "I love you."

Her eyes glistened, and she swallowed, letting out a low moan as I dragged the head of my cock through her folds again. With a sigh, she cupped my cheek. "I love you, Jesse..." she murmured.

We held still for a few beats, the air weighted with need and intimacy. When I sank inside of her, it felt like coming home. Her slick channel drew me inside, pulsing around me as I sank to the hilt, right where I belonged.

My forehead fell to hers. Sliding my hand free from her hair, I stroked down her back to grip her hips. We rocked into each other, every stroke spinning me tighter and tighter as she arched into me.

I was close to the edge already, the intensity of my impending release building rapidly. Reaching between us, I pressed my thumb to her clit, swirling over the swollen button of need, watching as her gaze darkened and then her head fell back with a loud cry. Her body shuddered as her channel clamped down around my cock.

That was all I needed, and my release crashed over me, pleasure whipping through me. The feel of her against me was the anchor in the storm. I held her tight as the crash of waves slowly receded. She curled against me, tucking her head into my shoulder.

My breath was still coming in rough gasps when she spoke. One of her hands slid up my back, her fingertips teasing the hair at the nape of my neck and sending spikes of pleasure through me.

"I missed you," she said softly. "I didn't really think that was possible when it's only been a little while."

Drawing back, I absorbed the sight of her – her cheeks flushed, her lips swollen, and her hair a tangled mess. "I know. I missed you too."

A little while later, after we'd put our clothes back on and I'd let Waffle inside to feed her, I glanced over at Charlie. "Do you need to get home soon?"

"I do. I can't exactly call Rachel to check in because she took my phone," she said with a sheepish smile.

"I'll walk you over. How about that?"

"Can you stay?"

Her question startled me, and it must've shown on my face. Her cheeks flushed, and she shrugged. "Em already called me out on us. I think she can deal just fine with you being there, and Mom would love it."

That night, I got to fall asleep with Charlie. I woke in the darkness with her warm against my side.

EPILOGUE

Charlie

More than a year later

The wind gusted across the parking lot behind Willow Brook Fire & Rescue. It was a rainy, windy day, and I was relieved to know Jesse's crew was still coming home today. I'd been worried the weather would delay him another day or two.

I knew he loved his job. Because it was such a part of him and who he was, I loved it too. But that didn't mean I didn't miss him like crazy. He'd been gone for three weeks now. Fire season this year in Alaska was busy. His crew had flown out to deal with a massive fire in the Alaskan Interior. The fire was moving toward Fairbanks and threatening a number of smaller communities along the way.

Whenever he was out at fires, he texted and called when he could, but that was maybe once a week at best. He was often completely out of cell range.

I hurried through the back door at the station, tossing my hood back. Giving my jacket a little shake to knock the rain off, I walked down the hallway toward the front. Pushing through the door, I smiled when I saw Em standing behind the counter, her head bent close to Maisie's. Maisie appeared to be showing her something on a clipboard.

Last year, which felt like forever ago at this point, Em had done her community service for getting caught smoking at school here at the station, as Jesse had suggested. She'd done such a good job that the Police Chief, Rex Masters, had offered her a part-time job.

Her job was essentially doing whatever nobody else had time for. This ranged from filing and helping Maisie in dispatch to cleaning the fire trucks and organizing equipment. Her current dream job was to become a hotshot firefighter. I wasn't quite sure how I felt about that, if only because it wasn't the safest option.

Considering that she was also pretty much the unofficial little sister of every guy on the three crews here and looked up to them, I was fairly certain that was the direction her career would take. We still had our bumpy days, but her job was one of the brightest spots in her life. I would support whatever she wanted and tuck my worries away.

Maisie glanced up first to see me. "Hey, Charlie, I wondered if you got my message earlier."

Em glanced up, giving me a little wave and then turning to the file cabinet behind Maisie.

"Of course I did. I was so busy, I didn't bother calling. I figured I'd just come over when you said they were due back. Any updates?"

Maisie shook her head, her dark curls swinging with the motion. Em turned back, closing the file cabinet as she did. "No updates, Aunt Charlie. Don't worry though, Jesse will be home soon," she said with a grin.

She'd been teasing me last night that I was moping about too much while he'd been gone. In the year plus that had passed since Jesse and I had finally managed to face what we meant to each other, a lot had happened. My mom was doing okay, and we'd moved into Jesse's place after the lease next door had expired.

My mom had seemed to stabilize in her state. She was still incredibly forgetful, but it didn't seem to be getting any worse. Despite all of my worries about what it would mean to try to bring a man into my life in a serious way, Jesse had been a stabilizing factor.

Maisie, who'd become a good friend over the past year, had pointed out once that perhaps I wasn't worried so much because I wasn't dealing with everything alone. We'd also had time to adjust to being here in Willow Brook. It felt like we were moving past those difficult years before we came here. Em was still a typical teenager and could still be cranky and sullen, more so with me. But that was okay.

Em rolled her eyes when all I did was shrug at her comment. "I need to go help Rex with some filing. Georgie's going to give me a ride home later, okay?"

She was referring to Rex's wife who often gave Em rides home due to her work schedule. They lived just beyond our road, so it wasn't out of her way. When I needed to work later, it was incredibly helpful. I didn't need to work late today, but I certainly wouldn't mind the free time with Jesse. Three weeks apart had more than my heart missing him.

"Of course, it's okay. I'll see you when you get home," I said as she turned away, pushing through another door that led to the police station side of the building.

Leaning against the counter, I glanced to Maisie. "I bet you're glad Beck will be home."

"Oh God, you have no idea. I know he loves his job, but I miss him when he's gone. I don't realize how much he helps out with the kids until he's not there."

"Well, it's not like you've ever complained about him not helping," I offered.

Maisie smiled ruefully. "I know, but you know how it is."

Beck's crew had been called out to the same fire as Jesse's, and they were due back together today.

"Speaking of kids, Lucy seems pretty excited," I added.

Maisie grinned widely. "I know. She was so wishy-washy about whether she wanted kids. Now that she's pregnant, she can't wait. What about you?"

I hoped my cheeks didn't get pink because I was currently holding onto a secret—one that I couldn't wait to share with Jesse. Until he knew, I didn't want to tell anyone else. Staying quiet was no easy feat because Maisie was a good friend now. I played it casual and simply shrugged. "I dunno. In my case, I dove into the thick of parenting with Em."

"Em is a *great* kid," Maisie said emphatically.

"I know she is."

We heard the distinct sound of a helicopter in the distance. Maisie quickly tapped a few keys and called into the Anchorage station to ask them to cover dispatch for a while. We hurried out together to the back of the station where the landing pad for the helicopter was on the far side of the parking lot.

With the rain coming down and the wind gusting, the helicopter landed slowly, jostling slightly as it settled to the ground. Maisie and I stayed back, waiting as the crewmembers filed off.

Jesse came out last, right behind Beck. Ella arrived just as Caleb was getting off with them. She gave a holler through the rain. Yet, the three of us weren't much for chatting, not right now.

My eyes honed in on Jesse like a beacon. He strolled across the pavement, swinging his bag over his shoulder. He swatted at the rain as if he could make it stop. His mouth curled up at one corner as he got closer and then he jogged the last bit of distance to reach me, sweeping me up against him with one arm.

With the rain falling, I tucked my head against his neck and breathed him in. He smelled of smoke and wilderness and rain. Leaning back, still held fast in his grip, I brushed his damp hair back.

"Missed you," he murmured as he caught my lips in a kiss.

In a flash, his tongue swept against mine, and our kiss got hot before I drew back with a laugh. "You know we're standing out in the rain with an audience?"

He chuckled. "I don't care."

"Let's go," I said, shimmying down from his hold.

We walked straight to his truck, which I'd driven over. Even though he was weary after three weeks of working one of the hardest jobs in the world, he still opened the door for me. Every time it made my heart squeeze.

"Is Emily here?" he asked.

"She is, but Georgie's bringing her home."

"Be right back. Just want to say hi first."

He closed the door, muting the sound of the rain failing. I couldn't even say what it meant to me how he'd taken Em into his life. He treated her like his daughter. Seeing as she'd never really had a father, it was something special for her.

JESSE

Later that night, Charlie cried out, her channel clenching as my release crashed over me. She fell against me, her body warm and soft, and her skin damp against mine. Catching my breath, I slid one hand up her spine and toyed with the ends of her hair.

Yet again, I'd had the best homecoming ever. I was coming to learn the sweetest part about being gone was coming home —because I came home to Charlie, Emily, Olive, and Waffle. Today had been even sweeter because I'd found out Charlie was pregnant. We'd decided to play it by ear only a few months ago. She'd had her IUD removed and told me not to get too excited because she wasn't young anymore at thirty-two. I turned the idea of a baby around in my thoughts. No doubt any baby of ours would be a handful, seeing as Charlie could be as stubborn and even more strong-willed than me. I couldn't wait.

My house was nothing like it had been a year ago, but I wouldn't trade it for a second. Life was complicated and sometimes messy, but I had Charlie and that was all that mattered. Funny thing was, as our lives had twined together like vines, the things she had worried were complications only made us stronger. I'd thought Charlie was all I wanted. But now I considered Em my daughter in every way that counted, and Olive, sweet, forgetful and occasionally sly, was a gift to have around.

My mom came over often and helped out with Olive when we needed it. Olive still went to the day groups, so she had her own world outside of our circle. Back when I'd come to terms with my feelings for Charlie, I'd thought it was simpler than that. I hadn't realized that in loving her, I would fall in love with her whole family.

I felt her lift her head, curling her hand into a fist and resting her chin on it. Opening my eyes, I collided with her smoky gray gaze, and my heart gave a thump. She'd owned my heart from the beginning.

"I'm glad you're home," she said softly.

"Ditto. You've completely worn me out now," I said with a chuckle. "I was so damn tired on the flight back today that I figured I wouldn't even have it in me."

"Well, it's been three weeks. You've got some work to do to make up for lost time," she replied with a sly grin.

I slowly shifted up on the pillows. She rose with me until she was straddling me as I leaned against the headboard. I'd been thinking a lot while I was gone. With my heart pounding and emotion tightening my chest, my eyes caught on the streak of purple in her hair. My heart saw that as a sign. That was something she and Emily did together every month. Emily had added two more streaks last time.

"So, I've been thinking," I said. She shifted her hips, her

channel clenching around me, actually sending a slide of need through me again. It was a damn miracle under the circumstances.

"About what?" she asked, her voice husky.

I'd meant for this to be more romantic than this, but then I supposed it was romantic to be as physically intimate as we could possibly be at the moment.

"I want to marry you."

My words fell into the quiet room. The intake of her breath was audible. I suddenly got nervous, wondering if I taken it a step too far ahead.

But then tears rolled down her cheeks, and she nodded rapidly. "Yes, yes, yes." She paused. "Wait, was that a question?"

At my nod, she dusted kisses over my face and then leaned back, cocking her head to the side. "This is going to make Em's year."

"Really?"

She nodded. "She worries you know. Her dad was never around, so every so often she'll ask me about you and about us. Nothing big, just little questions."

"Well, that leads me to the next thing," I paused to take a breath. "I want you to know whatever you think is best is what I want to do."

Charlie nodded slowly. "Okay, what is it?"

"Emily is like a daughter to me. I know that when her mom arranged the adoption for you to go through that her father relinquished his rights. So if Emily wanted it, I'd make it official and adopt her too. I don't want her to think..."

I didn't get to finish because Charlie was crying all over again.

"Is this good or bad?" I asked after a moment, uncertain how to interpret her reaction.

Charlie leaned back, brushing her tears away. "It's good. You're the only father she's ever had. Except for her grand-dad. I think you should ask her without me around. I don't want her to look to me about what she thinks I might want. I want it to be her answer."

"That scares the shit out of me," I said flatly.

Charlie burst out laughing before leaning forward and catching my lips in a soft kiss. "If you can handle me, you can handle her."

I fell asleep with Charlie held tight against my side. The next morning, I took Emily out for coffee and she cried too. But it was all good.

Family was messy. Life was messy. Later that night, when I looked across the table at Charlie and her violet gray gaze caught mine, I might as well have just handed her my heart.

———

Thank you for reading Sweet Fire - I hope you loved Jesse & Charlie's story!

Up next in the Into the Fire Series is Play With Fire - Jasmine & Donovan's story. They meet, ahem, after Jasmine starts a bar fight. Donovan takes tall dark & sexy to new heights & finds himself drawn to fiery Jasmine in ways he never imagined. Don't miss Donovan's story!

Keep reading for a sneak peek!

Be sure to sign up for my newsletter for the latest news, teasers & more! Click here to sign up: http://jhcroixauthor.com/subscribe/

EXCERPT: PLAY WITH FIRE

DONOVAN

Leaning against the bar at Wildlands Lodge, I took a long pull on my beer and scanned the bar and restaurant. It was a busy night here, but then even a slow night was crowded. I was tucked into a corner with a good view of the room. As I glanced around, my gaze landed on a woman playing pool in the corner nearby.

I idly wondered if she was a tourist. Willow Brook, Alaska was a small town, yet it was smack in the middle of summer, which meant the town was teeming with tourists. Pushing off the bar, as if drawn by an actual force, I found myself walking in her direction.

Her dark golden hair glinted under the dim lighting in the bar. It fell down her back in a cascade, almost reaching her waist. With a flick of her hand, she brushed it over her shoulder as I approached. She wore jeans and cowboy boots paired with a loose red blouse. Somehow, hell if I knew how, I knew there were curves to die for hidden behind that silk.

She was in the midst of a game with several men and

looked well on her way to being tipsy. While I'd initially walked over here without thinking much about it, as I got close, I noticed the hum of tension in the air. Two of the men near the table were leering at her.

There were different kinds of men. It was one thing to appreciate a woman—hell, that was what I'd been doing—and it was another thing to look at them as if you could do whatever the hell you wanted. I felt as if I'd walked into a pack of dogs jockeying for position. To make matters worse, this woman wasn't paying the least bit of attention to it. She was focused on the game. My hackles rose.

As she leaned over to make a shot, one of the men slid his hand over her ass. In a flash, she spun around, pulled her fist back and clocked him right in the nose.

"Get your hands off of me!" she declared, swinging her pool stick in his direction.

She clearly didn't need help.

"What the fuck?!" The guy who'd been the recipient of her fist wiped blood off of his nose.

"Don't grab my fucking ass," the woman said.

One of the other guys snickered. "Well, sweets, you can't just waltz in here and show off your ass like that."

"Oh hell fucking no," the woman said.

I threaded through the cluster around her. I didn't even know who she was, but I needed to get her out of the middle of this mess.

"I'm playing pool. That doesn't give any of you idiots the right to touch me," the woman said, swinging her pool stick around again.

I caught the end of it and tugged it out of her hands. While I'd be happy to watch her whack few of these assholes, it might not work out in her favor. Glancing around at the guys, I said, "Okay, boys, break it up."

"Hey, she fucking hit me," the man with the bloody nose retorted.

"Yeah, well you grabbed her ass, and she didn't appreciate it. So, like I said, back the fuck off."

The bartender, Mike Morgan, stepped to my side and leaned over. "Heads up, but that's Levi Phillips's sister. She drove here, so I'm about to take her keys. Mind giving her a ride home?"

Aw fuck. Levi was a friend of mine. We were both firefighters at Willow Brook Fire & Rescue. I wasn't so sure I wanted to be the one giving his sister a ride home, but more than that, I didn't want to see her caught in the middle of this.

"Not a problem," I replied, glancing to Mike. "I'll call Levi once we get her out of here."

Mike waded into the cluster. Mike dealt with the guys, while I stepped to Jasmine's side. Just as I was about to open my mouth, she spun to look at the guy who'd copped a feel. "And don't grab my ass again."

With a huff, she spun back to face me. Sweet hell. She was fucking beautiful. Her cheeks were flushed, and her eyes snapping fire. My body had all kinds of thoughts about her. She was flat out gorgeous with that fall of honey hair and deep sapphire eyes.

Before I had a chance to speak, Mike stopped in front of Jasmine. "Hand them over," he said, holding his palm out.

"Hand what over?" Jasmine asked, narrowing her eyes at Mike.

"Your keys. This is Donovan Ryan if you haven't met him before. He works with Levi, and he's giving you a ride home," Mike explained matter-of-factly.

"What the hell?" Jasmine asked, her gaze bouncing between us.

"Look, you've already hit one guy. You're drunk, and you're not driving anywhere," Mike said flatly.

Jasmine, glanced between Mike and me, clearly not pleased with this turn of events. After a taut moment, she shook her head. "No, I don't need a ride."

Mike wasn't moved in the slightest. "You climb behind the wheel of your car, and I won't hesitate to call the police. They can probably walk here faster than you can back out of a parking spot," he said, not even the least bit ruffled by how pissed off she seemed. "Way I see it, you've got three choices. One – ride home with Donovan. Two — I call Levi and he'll come get you. Three – the guy you hit might actually decide to call the police because you hit him. Take your pick."

Jasmine rolled her eyes and sighed. "Fine. Do I have to give you my keys if he gives me a ride?" she countered, thumbing in my direction.

When Mike shook his head, she turned her attention to me. "Nice to meet you, Donovan."

I simply nodded, busy trying to tell my body not to notice the fact that she was hot as hell.

Mike cocked his head to the side. "So you're riding with Donovan?"

Jasmine nodded and then spun around, stalking across the floor ahead of me.

"Looks like I'm outta here," I said with a chuckle.

"Levi will appreciate it," Mike murmured as I walked past him.

Jasmine's hair swung just above her hips as she threaded her way through the tables before disappearing down a hallway in the back. I caught up to her quickly, reaching her just as she stumbled slightly in the hallway when she tried to dodge a group of people walking in from the parking lot.

"Dammit," she muttered under her breath.

I caught her elbow to steady her. The moment she shook me loose, she promptly stumbled again, bouncing into the wall. Leaning against it, she rolled both shoulders against the wall, eyeing me. Her dark blue gaze swept up and down my body.

"Damn, you're handsome," she said, her mouth lifting at the corner in a slow grin.

I took a breath and kept my eyes focused on her face. "You like to swear when you're drunk," I countered.

I was acutely aware of the shadowed valley between her breasts with her red silk blouse slipping and sliding when she lifted a hand to brush a loose lock of hair out of her eyes.

"What the hell is wrong with swearing?" she asked.

"Nothing at all. Just seems like you can't say a sentence without swearing."

Jasmine stared at me, her rich blue gaze assessing. "You must be new to Willow Brook. I don't think I know you."

"Depends on what you mean by new. I moved here about two years ago when I joined a hotshot crew. That's how I know Levi. How about we get going?"

Jasmine eyed me for another few beats and then shrugged, pushing away from the wall. When I lightly gripped her elbow this time, she didn't shrug me off. We stepped out into the cool summer air. It was going on 9 PM, the sun only now making its final bow for the night, leaving a crescent of orange just above the mountains in the distance. The sky was streaked with orange, red, and gold.

Jasmine came to a quick stop when we were about halfway through the parking lot. She lifted her head and took a deep breath, letting it out with a gusty sigh. "I love the air here. It's the best air," she murmured softly, the edges of her voice soft.

The summer air was earthy, scented with spruce and the crispness of the mountains surrounding us. Swan Lake stretched out in front of us just beyond the cars in the parking lot behind the lodge.

Jasmine looked toward me, her gaze considering. "I bet you're not an asshole," she said flatly.

"I'd like to think not," I offered, uncertain where this topic was headed.

The anger, bravado, and recklessness with which she'd carried herself up to this point disappeared in a flash. It was as if she was deflated by nothing more than a thought.

After her announcement, she stepped closer. Before I even realized what the hell she was doing, she leaned up, slipped her hand around my nape and kissed me. For a flash, I was so startled I didn't even move, and then her mouth was moving over mine, and I reacted.

Threading a hand into her glorious hair, I tugged her to me and swiped my tongue across the seam of her lips. She moaned into my mouth, the sound nudging me back to sanity. I tore my lips free and gave my head a shake.

"What the hell was that?"

She smiled, her eyes glittering. "I couldn't help it. Your mouth is too damn sexy."

At that, she traced my lips with her fingertip, the feel of her touch like fire.

"You're gonna have to take me to Levi's," she announced next as her hand fell away.

"I'll drive you wherever you need to go. Come on," I said, turning away because I couldn't keep looking at her and not want to kiss her again.

She walked along with me, her stride slower now. She gave off a sense of weariness and sadness. Once we were situated in my truck, she let out a deep sigh and leaned her head back against the seat.

"Levi doesn't know I'm here by the way," she murmured.

Great, just great. I was going to take her to Levi's, but I had a feeling that there was some kind of story behind why she was here, and I had no idea what it was.

All I knew was Jasmine was beautiful, she drew me to her like a fucking magnet, and the second her vulnerability flashed in her eyes, I wanted to take care of her. That was a dangerous feeling.

I knew where Levi lived, so I simply started driving in that direction. Jasmine was sound asleep by the time I arrived at Levi's place. I climbed quietly out of the truck, I considering whether I should go knock, or carry her in.

Glancing at the darkened windows of Levi's home, I realized I'd likely be waking him and Lucy up as it was. Rounding to the passenger side, I opened the door. Carrying the delectable Jasmine Phillips was not something I wanted to do, or rather it was something I definitely wanted, so that wasn't smart. Steeling myself, I reached around her to unbuckle her seat belt, gritting my teeth when she sighed softly in her sleep.

Her body was warm and lush. I could feel her lithe build and the soft curve of one of her breasts against my chest. Fuck me. I ordered my cock down and walked swiftly to the door. After a quick knock, I waited. Several moments passed before Levi answered, a look of confusion on his face. "What are you doing here? And what the hell is Jasmine doing with you?"

"Short version—she was at Wildlands, the bartender took her keys and asked me to take her home."

All in all, that summed it up nicely, minus the messy details.

Levi's eyes widened as he ran a hand through his rumpled hair. He and Jasmine shared the same coloring—honey blond hair and blue eyes. It was obvious I'd woken him up. "What the hell?" he finally muttered.

"Yeah, she mentioned you didn't know she was here."

Levi looked completely flummoxed, but he nodded and opened the door, gesturing me through. With Levi pointing the way, I carried Jasmine to the couch and set her down. Between her unexpected kiss and the way it felt to hold her in my arms, I was doing battle with the state of my body.

I followed Levi into the kitchen. "Thanks, man. Anything I should know about?"

Standing there, I contemplated whether it would be better if he heard from me that Jasmine hauled off and punched a guy who grabbed her ass, or through the grapevine.

I decided hearing it from me was better. "Well, the

bartender asked me to take her home after some guy grabbed her ass, and she hauled off and punched him."

Levi's eyes widened and then he shook his head slowly back and forth. "Do you happen to know who the asshole was?"

"Nope. She can hold her own though."

"Oh, she can," he said with a wry chuckle. "Thanks for bringing her home."

"Not a problem. See you at the station."

Driving home through the falling darkness, the only thing my mind tripped over was the feel of Jasmine's lips against mine. With a hard shake I forced my attention off of her, watching as the moon rose ahead in the sky, stars claiming the fading light.

JASMINE

Bright light woke me, the sun warm on my face. Ugh. My head was pounding. It took me a moment to get my bearings. Opening my eyes slowly, first one and then the other, I glanced around, realizing that I was in Levi and Lucy's guest bedroom. I was fully dressed with my blouse twisted around my waist.

My mind flashed back to the evening before. A man, a classically handsome, tall, dark, and sexy-as-fucking-hell man had driven me here last night.

For the life of me, I couldn't remember his name. But I had a crystal clear picture of what he looked like and the way his mouth felt against mine.

I flung my arm over my face, my cheeks getting hot. Said man had almost black hair and rich hazel eyes. I remembered looking into them, the layered colors of green and gold mingled with nutmeg. His face had clean lines—sculpted cheekbones, a square jaw, a slightly crooked nose as if he'd been in a fight, and a sensual mouth with a dimple in the center of his chin.

Even though my memories were blurry, I recalled that he'd made me feel safe. As mortified as I was that I'd kissed him, I was positive I'd seen a flicker of desire in his eyes.

Who the hell was he?

I'd have to figure that out later. For now I had to sort out who I would be facing here. I wasn't quite ready to face my brother Levi, especially not with a hangover. I adored Levi, but he could be overprotective. I'd come home unexpectedly without any advance warning, so I knew there would be questions. Levi thought I was too wild, too reckless, or so he'd said once upon a time. I hoped my options were no one, or my sister-in-law Lucy. I could handle Lucy.

I slowly dragged my arm away from my face and rubbed my eyes with my fists. Moving carefully and trying not to jostle my pounding head too much, I swung my feet over the side of the bed and straightened up gingerly.

Opening the door crack, I listened to see if I could hear any voices. Silence greeted me, so I pulled the door open and walked toward the bathroom. I paused for a moment when I rounded the edge of the balcony upstairs. I loved this house. Levi had built it himself. The upstairs had a balcony that followed three sides of the house with windows from below extending to the upper floor in the front of the house.

Mist rose off the field outside with the sun angling across the dew-covered grasses and flowers in the field. The home offered a view of a field with a small pond to the side. Spruce and birch trees were scattered in the field and gradually thickened into forest with the mountains rising tall in the distance. My heart gave a hard thump. Alaska was home to me, and my heart knew it.

Over the balcony railing, I could look into the living room. As far as I could tell, it appeared no one else was here. With a sigh, I shuffled into the bathroom and paused to take a look at myself. My dark blond hair was a tousled mess, and my cheek had an imprint of the wrinkled sheets against it. My eyes were puffy and bleary.

In short, I looked like hell. I could only hope that when I'd made a pass at *tall dark, and sexy* last night, I hadn't looked this bad. I was about to strip out of my clothes when I saw a note taped on the shelf by the shower in front of a clean stack of towels.

Morning, Jasmine. Levi's off at the station, and I'm out on a few errands. Here's a change of clothes. I'll see you when I get back. To start the coffee, just turn it on. There are bagels and cream cheese in the fridge. We missed you. Glad you're here.

Lucy

PS: Levi's wondering what the hell is going on. We hope you're OK. Love you.

I started laughing. Because what else was there to do? Lucy was the best sister-in-law. She was also sarcastic and kind of quirky, which made her even better.

Peeling out of my clothes, I climbed in the shower, sighing at the feel of the hot water pouring over me. That alone eased my headache a bit.

As I showered, a few more memories filtered in from last night. Specifically, the idiot who grabbed my ass and then I punched him.

Great, just great. I couldn't wait to hear what Levi had to say about that.

After I showered, I downed two ibuprofen I found in the medicine cabinet and made my way downstairs in the clothes Lucy had left for me. She was smaller than me, but she tended to wear loose clothes. Her comfy sweatpants and T-shirt fit just fine.

Seeing as I couldn't go anywhere, it didn't really matter how I looked. After I started the coffee, toasted a bagel and slathered it with cream cheese, I sat down at the kitchen table to eat. I felt halfway human after some coffee and a few bites of my bagel.

The tension bundled inside of me started to ease slowly. The problem with that was I wanted to cry. Five days ago, I stopped by my apartment to pick up my lunch after I forgot to bring it to work. My life in San Francisco consisted of working my ass off at a pottery cooperative because I loved it and working at an art gallery to make ends meet. I worked insane hours and was rarely home during weekdays.

When I'd arrived at the apartment I shared with my now ex-fiancé, I'd been puzzled when I heard a thumping sound. Because I could be a spectacular idiot sometimes, I followed the sound, right to our bedroom. Even then, I didn't get suspicious. It was only when I started to open the door that a cold prickle ran up my spine and my gut clenched.

That moment of tension was followed by a bolt of anger. The door swung fully open, and I was greeted with a sight of Glen—my now ex-fiancé—on his back with the assistant manager from the gallery where I worked straddling him. To say they were going to town might've been an understatement.

That thumping sound? That was the headboard hitting the wall over and over and over again. She was gripping it with her hands, so every time she moved, it bounced against the wall. I was in such shock, I just stood there watching them. I oddly tried to recall the last time Glen and I had sex and thought maybe it was about three weeks.

I'd chalked it up to being too busy. We both had crazy schedules and sometimes passed like ships in the night for days at a time. In the throes of their rather enthusiastic fucking, it took them a moment or two to notice my presence.

Lisa, my now former assistant manager, looked over her shoulder. "Oh shit!"

She started to move, but I was surprisingly calm. "Just carry on. I won't be hanging around."

I walked out of the room, calling over my shoulder, "Be out of here within an hour. I'll be back to get my stuff and I don't want to see either one of you."

Thinking back, I couldn't quite believe I managed to

think at all. I heard Glen scrambling off the bed and his footsteps.

"Jasmine, it's not what you think!"

I spun back to find him hurrying out of the bedroom, wrapping a sheet around his waist. I'd taken a moment to stare at him. "There's not much to think about for me to interpret what I just saw. We're done."

Tears were threatening, and I wasn't about to let them see me fall apart. I clung to my anger like a shield. Because it was all I had. "Be out of here in an hour."

He hurried after me, but I left, slamming the door in his face.

That was five days ago. He'd had the decency to be gone when I came back. I'd packed all of my clothes, took all of my pottery and put it in my car, and left. I'd spent the night with another friend and then came home. I'd considered staying, but I managed to get myself fired on the same day.

I had a bit of a temper sometimes. That same afternoon, it wasn't a shocker that I was in a pissy mood at the gallery after my lunch break. Working in an art gallery wasn't really a great fit for my personality, but I'd needed the money.

I preferred to have my hands dirty while throwing pottery, not dolling myself up and being polite and gracious to the rich people who would spend money on art. I'd been a little emotionally overwhelmed and so out of sorts inside that I'd publicly confronted Lisa when she returned to the gallery in front of a customer. I couldn't believe she'd had the nerve, but then she was a step above me there. The manager didn't appreciate me calling her second-in-command a whore. She'd fired me on the spot No job, no fiancé, and no money.

I hadn't been thinking it through, but the next morning, I'd pointed my car north and driven home to Alaska. It took me four days to get here.

Just now, emotion finally pushed through that shield of anger, the cracks in it spreading rapidly. Hot tears rolled down my cheeks as I cried, so hard I was hiccupping. Trying to catch my breath, I felt a tickle on my foot. Glancing down, my brother's hamster, aptly named Ham, was sniffing at my feet. Brown and white, little Ham looked up at me as if he somehow understood how upset I was. I sniffled, dragging my sleeve across my face, and managed to smile at Ham. Leaning over, I stroked my fingertips across his back. He sniffed my hand and then scurried away.

I watched as he climbed up a step stool that Levi left there for him to scurry across the windowsill into a little pillow bed. Only my brother, my hotshot firefighter, badass brother, would have a hamster he let run loose in the house and treated like a king.

My tears subsided. I didn't like thinking about all the reasons why I was back in Willow Brook. I took a sip of my coffee and wondered what my next steps were. Because I'd come here in a huff and had no plan. For a huff, I sure had to drive a long damned way to get here.

I'd left Willow Brook straight out of high school. I wanted to see the bigger world. I had landed in San Francisco. I loved many aspects of San Francisco—the hum and busyness of the big city, the eclectic mix of people, the quaint buildings, and the art, so much art. I'd finished college and started working at a studio, falling in love with making pottery. There were some things I hadn't loved so much though. For example, apparently lots of people were gluten sensitive and most of them were vegan. I loved bread and I ate meat, and I didn't intend to change that anytime soon.

I never quite felt like I fit in. I was perhaps too rough around the edges, definitely not glamorous enough. While I wasn't a full on tomboy, I definitely bordered on it. I preferred to wear jeans and boots and T-shirts while I worked, dressing up only when necessary. Cowboy boots were practically uniform for me.

I'd also missed Alaska. Once the novelty of seeing the

wider world had worn off, there was always a little ache in my heart—longing for the midnight sun of summer days, the crisp snowy nights, and the sense of feeling like I belonged no matter who I was.

That was a funny quality here. Alaska was so filled with transplants that you could find every kind of person. There were plenty of gluten-free vegans, but they rubbed shoulders with the fishermen and hunters and then some. There was a high tolerance for *to each their own* here.

And, oh my God, I'd missed the view. Just now, looking out over the field outside the kitchen window, that tight ball of tension and hurt eased. Oddly, I was more hurt by Lisa's actions than Glen's. While she'd sort of been my boss, until the other day, I'd have considered her a friend.

That was like a rule, right? You didn't fuck your friend's fiancé.

———

Available now!
Play With Fire

If you love steamy, small town romance, take a visit to Diamond Creek, Alaska in my Last Frontier Lodge Series. A sexy, alpha SEAL meets his match with a brainy heroine in Take Me Home. Don't miss Gage & Marley's story!

Go here to sign up for information on new releases: http://jhcroixauthor.com/subscribe/

Burn For Me
Slow Burn
Burn So Bad
Hot Mess
Burn So Good
Sweet Fire
Play With Fire
Melt With You
Burn For You
Crash & Burn
Swoon Series
This Crazy Love
Wait For Me
Break My Fall
Brit Boys Sports Romance
The Play
Big Win
Out Of Bounds
Play Me
Naughty Wish
Diamond Creek Alaska Novels
When Love Comes
Follow Love
Love Unbroken
Love Untamed
Tumble Into Love
Christmas Nights
Last Frontier Lodge Novels
Take Me Home
Love at Last
Just This Once
Falling Fast
Stay With Me
When We Fall
Hold Me Close
Crazy For You

Catamount Lion Shifters

Protected Mate

Chosen Mate

Fated Mate

Destined Mate

A Catamount Christmas

Ghost Cat Shifters

The Lion Within

Lion Lost & Found

ACKNOWLEDGMENTS

This story goes out to my late editor, Laura Kingsley. Her sharp comments on story, character development, and more helped me learn so much over the last few years. She handed this one back to me the same week I learned she passed away unexpectedly. My heart goes out to her family.

Even though her part was done, and this story was on the way to the proofreader, I fretted. She tore my work apart time and again and became a friend in the process. As is so often the case, we don't realize how much we rely on someone until they aren't there. She's not here to read this, and I don't quite know how to show my gratitude. These two words will have to do: thank you.

My proofreader angels catch anything that gets by - Janine, Beth P., Terri D., Terri E., Heather H., & Carolyne B. - a bow of thanks. Yoly Cortez spun magic with this cover once again.

My husband makes sure I laugh. Or rather, I should say he makes it impossible not to laugh. My dogs - always there in heart and soul.

xoxo
J.H. Croix

ABOUT THE AUTHOR

USA Today Bestselling Author J. H. Croix lives in a small town in the historical farmlands of Maine with her husband and two spoiled dogs. Croix writes contemporary romance with sassy women and alpha men who aren't afraid to show some emotion. Her love for quirky small-towns and the characters that inhabit them shines through in her writing. Take a walk on the wild side of romance with her bestselling novels!

Places you can find me:
jhcroixauthor.com
jhcroix@jhcroix.com

facebook.com/jhcroix

twitter.com/jhcroix